Angela Huth has written th: and several novels, includir is *Drowning*, *South of the Lignts*, *invitation to the Married Life* and *Land Girls*. She also writes plays for radio, television and stage, and is a well-known freelance journalist, critic and broadcaster. She is married to a don, lives in Oxford and has two daughters.

Another Kind of Cinderella

and Other Stories

ANGELA HUTH

An *Abacus* Book

First published in Great Britain by Little, Brown 1996
Published by Abacus 1997

The following stories have previously been published:
Another Kind of Cinderella' in *Winter's Tales*; 'Dressing Up' in
the *Daily Telegraph*; 'Mothers and Fathers' on *BBC Morning
tory*; 'To Re-Arrange a Room' in *Marie Claire*; 'The Wife Trap'
in *Raconteur*, 'Squirrels' in *Winter's Tales*; 'Mistral' in the *New
Yorker*; 'Men Friends' on *BBC Morning Story*.

A CIP catalogue record for this book
is available from the British Library.

ISBN 0 349 10766 1

Typeset in Berkeley by M Rules
Printed and bound in Great Britain by
Clays Ltd, St Ives plc

Abacus
A Division of
Little, Brown and Company (UK)
Brettenham House
Lancaster Place
London WC2E 7EN

For my mother

Contents

Another Kind

of Cinderella

'Now come along, gentlemen, *if* you please,' urged Lewis Crone, waving his baton. 'What we want is a little more *up*lift in the last bar, don't we? Up, up and *away*.'

'Stuff it, Lew,' murmured Reginald Breen, second violinist, under his breath.

He dabbed at the sweat on his forehead with a large white handkerchief. It was bloody hot down here in the pit, even in winter. And he was damned if he'd give the last bar a lift. It wasn't exactly Beethoven the Winterstown Concert Orchestra was struggling to bring some life to, after all. Just wallpaper music to fill the gap where the Fairy blooming Godmother turned the mice into ponies. They hadn't half had some trouble with the ponies this year, what's more – doing their business just at the wrong moment, and so on. Reginald sniffed.

'So once again, gentlemen,' the mighty Lewis, conductor with airs above his station, was saying. 'We'll take it once again, *if* you please.'

What's the point, Reginald wondered, being this particular for this kind of show? Not a soul in the audience would notice whether or not there was a wretched uplift in the last bar. Half of them would be under twelve. The other half, pensioners' outings, were plugged into hearing aids.

For them a pantomime was no different from a silent film. He tucked his instrument under his chin, and turned with an exaggerated look of scorn to his friend, Tom, first violin.

'Better give it the works,' whispered Tom, 'or he'll keep us into the dinner hour.'

'Righty-ho. Last time. Up, up and *away*.' Reginald had perfected his mimicry over the years.

He and Tom lifted their bows in unison. Tom caught the conductor's agitated eye. The orchestra crashed once more into the last few lines of forgettable music. Their sudden energy came from indignation. Lewis Crone had kept them at it since ten this morning. They were now hungry, bored and fed up with his absurd attention to detail. Trouble was, Lewis had once seen André Previn rehearsing an orchestra on television. Since then he had applied his own version of Previn's methods to the WCO, causing much suffering and discontent. In the old days they'd played through the score a couple of times at the beginning of the season – *Jack and the Beanstalk, Aladdin, Mother Goose,* whatever – and that was it. Now, all this pernickety fussing was driving them to near rebellion. Most of the players – weary, professional men – had considered resigning, but none actually did so. There were not many openings for their class of musician on the south coast. Tom was the most vociferous in his complaints. Reginald encouraged him in his discontent, for Tom's resignation would be to Reginald's own benefit. Once Tom had gone he, Reginald, would surely become first violin. He had waited some thirty years for this position. Over and over again others, outrageously, had been placed above him – incompetent musicians, mostly, from outside the orchestra. And once, worst of all, a very junior 'talented' violinist from the WCO itself. He hadn't lasted long: no stamina. Many times Reginald had suffered the humiliation of being passed over, and had kept his silence and his hope. He could not afford to resign.

The morning's rehearsal over, Tom and Reginald made their way along the front. They exchanged few words: music was their only common interest. Proper music. Tom carried his violin case under his arm. Home, this afternoon, Tom would be practising the Mozart concerto. Reginald would be attending to his mother.

The sea breeze on their faces was good after the stuffiness of the orchestra pit. Reginald always enjoyed the short walk home. It refreshed him, gave him strength for the tasks ahead.

'Still haven't got the coach finished, I hear,' said Tom.

'Coach and beanstalk, it's the same every year, always late.' Reginald smiled at the thought of the familiar incompetence.

'At least we'll see Valerie in her spangles, tomorrow.' Tom was something of a woman's man, keenly sensitive to the potential of leading ladies.

'She's as good a Cinderella as I can remember, I'll say that.' Reginald himself had been quite taken with her – what he could see from the pit – during the past month of rehearsals.

As the men parted, Tom paused for a last look out to sea. There was a small fishing boat on the horizon.

'Give anything to be out there,' he muttered, more to himself than to his friend. 'Always fancied playing on the deck of a boat, up and down in time with the waves.' He gave a small, helpless laugh. Reginald smiled in reply. He, too, had known fantasies that would never materialise.

He slowed his pace, once Tom had gone. He was always reluctant to return home and face *that* kind of music: but face it he must, as he told himself every day. If he didn't hurry and buy his mother her paper there would be more to answer for.

'Is that you, Reginald?'

The familiar peevish tone bit into his ears as soon as he was through the door. Who the hell do you think it is, he wanted to shout back. Who else would let themselves in at twelve fifty-five precisely, as he did five days a week?

'It's me, mother, all right,' he called, and clenched his fists, taking a grip on himself before going in to the front room.

Mrs Breen sat in an armchair in the bow window. Her vastly swollen legs hung from widely parted knees, slippered feet not quite touching the floor. A mustard crochet cardigan – made in the days when she still bothered to sew the crochet squares together – covered a bosom so cumbersome she was unable to see her own hands in its shade. But the fingers (the worst kind of sausages, Reginald thought, among other savage thoughts) worked skilfully on their own, crocheting away, square after square, hour after hour. The furious, pale eyes, scowling on their ledge of fat purple cheek, were attending to some cooking programme on the television. Mrs Breen had not moved since Reginald had left her that morning. She was not able to move on her own. Her illness meant she was almost completely immobile, though Reginald had reason to think that on secret occasions, when she wanted something badly enough, she was able to reach it. Chocolates in the tin on the bookshelf, for instance. Their unaccountable disappearance, observed by Reginald on many occasions when his mother was in bed, could only mean one thing. But the time had not yet come to challenge her.

Her mauvish bulk backlit by the netted light from the window, Mrs Breen made no effort to drag her eyes from the television.

'I fancy the Ambrosia today, Reginald,' she said, 'with that tin of plums you got last Friday.'

Incapable of shopping herself, her recall of exactly what her son had bought, when, was extraordinary. She would plan the life of half a pound of cheddar down to the last slice, insistent that only an ounce should be used for the sauce for the macaroni, and the merest scrapings for the Tuesday cheese supper with biscuits and tomatoes. Should Reginald miscalculate, and the cheese be finished before its allotted time, Mrs Breen would be moved to one of her famous rages when every blood vessel in her body enlarged, darkened, and threatened to burst through her glowering skin.

'Anything else?'

'Tin of curried spaghetti still there, is it?'

'It is.'

Reginald's heart pounded in relief. Last night he had had half a mind to eat it, but had resisted on the ground that he had had no energy to ask his mother's permission.

'Then I'll have that.'

Reginald went to the kitchen to set about opening tins and preparing the tray. The room faced north. Any light that managed to challenge the old curtain at the window was diffused by the coarse-grained and very dirty net. A smell of disinfectant clashed with the smells of years of frugal meals. Opening the window was forbidden, so the air was never cleared. The kitchen gave Reginald a headache every day. He dreaded it. But there was no escape. How many years, now? Eight? Almost nine. And how many more . . .?

When he had placed his mother's tray of lunch beside her, he returned to the kitchen. But he could not face either washing up last night's supper dishes and the breakfast, or making himself a sandwich. Instead, he went out into the strip of ill-kept grass that was the back garden. When his father had been alive, herbaceous borders ran down both sides – borders that kept the old man's every spare moment fully occupied. From the thin earth, he had managed to persuade a magnificent show of hollyhocks, tulips, dahlias (his speciality) – the lot. But Reginald could never be bothered with gardening. Everything had gone to seed, died off years ago. Now the lawn was bordered with weeds. But the apple tree, the single tree in the Breen family possession, still blossomed. And the blackbird still lived there. Reginald listened to its song now – vibrant, optimistic notes that gave him the courage to go on, sometimes. He lit a cigarette. Into his mind came a picture of Valerie, who in tomorrow's dress rehearsal would be in all her finery at the ball. He looked forward to that. He found himself pecking quite fast at the cigarette, then grinding its stub under his heel with a force that surprised him. Valerie was the sort of girl, had things been different, Reginald might well have approached. He had no great ambitions concerning her, of course, even in his imagination. With the difference in their ages, marriage was naturally out of the question. No: all he wanted, or told himself he wanted, was a friend. Her funny crooked smile and short bouncy hair inspired him with exciting ideas of friendship. Perhaps one day he would summon the courage to speak to her, see how things went.

'Reg! It's time.'

Reginald allowed himself a moment's more reflection, then returned to his mother. It was time for the dreaded visit to the bathroom, the ungainly negotiating of the dim passage, the old woman's entire weight on his arm, her invective spewing in his ear. Then, the long afternoon. He would have liked to go to his room, have another go at the Tchaikovsky. But his mother could hear, she said, however quietly he played. It hurt her ears, all that screeching, she said – she had always wanted Reginald to go into insurance, like his father. The violin was forbidden in the house.

Instead of music, it would be shopping at the Co-op, hoovering the stairs, two hours of bad-tempered Scrabble, another tray for high tea, television, and the terrible ritual of putting Mrs Breen to bed. By the time Reginald went to his own room he was exhausted. Like a disobedient child, he would play his radio under the bedclothes for a while, very loud. This was the part of the day he most looked forward to. Much though he enjoyed his nightly blast of illicit music, it put him to sleep almost at once.

*

On the noticeboard at the stage door it was announced that the transformation scene was the first to be rehearsed. Reginald felt a slight pricking of anticipation as he undid his violin case, took out the instrument and wiped its bow. The awkward notes of his fellow musicians, tuning up, usually filled him with gloom and unease as he faced the long morning of indifferent music ahead. Today the squawks of striving notes could not touch him. He tried out a few notes himself, tightened a couple of strings. He scarcely noticed Lewis Crone blundering up on the podium, cocky, grinning, one hand fingering a yellow tie.

'Making a statement, what?' whispered Tom, who was using a duster to polish his violin – a very superior instrument which could not have been better cared for had it been a Stradivarius.

'Won't get anywhere,' replied Reginald. He had no idea why he made this comment, or if there was any truth in his speculation.

The stage lights were switched on, bringing life to the Ugly Sisters' grim kitchen.

'Idiot,' yelled a voice from off-stage. 'That's the ballroom effing light.'

The peach light was dimmed, replaced by the kind of light usually glowing in the front room at Reginald's house. No wonder Cinderella, shortly to be sitting by the giant fireplace, needed a Fairy Godmother. Reginald could have done with one most days himself.

Bev Birley, in fishnet tights and a short satin tunic, came striding on to the stage. Bev was Prince Charming. Last year she had been Jack, the year before Aladdin. Beginning to show her years, too, thought Reginald, noting the definite thickness of her hips. He had never liked Bev – not that he had ever had occasion to talk to her. But she was stuck-up, haughty, tongue like a whiplash to junior members of the cast, though all agreeable smiles to visiting stars. Between seasons, Reginald saw her sometimes in the town walking a terrier. Once, he recognised her picture in the window of an optician. She was wearing flyaway blue-tinted glasses and her hair had been stuck down with grease. She still did not look very nice. Presumably, not being in national demand, she had to do any job she could to keep herself going between seasons.

'Anyone wanting me this morning?' Bev shouted into the darkness of the auditorium, legs spread wide, hands on hips, her annual stance in every proposal scene. There was a slight titter in the orchestra pit. Tom nodded towards Reginald. Bev scowled.

'No one wanting you till two, darling,' the director called from the back of the stalls. 'See you then.'

Bev stomped off.

'Stuck-up bit, know what I'd like to do to her,' whispered Tom.

Reginald had no time to imagine what this might be because Cinderella came on to the stage just then, wrapped in a large cloak. She wore a great deal of scarlet lipstick which made her crooked smile look very grown up. As Bev passed her, she whispered something that made them both smile, and ruffled her hair.

'Cheek,' said Tom.

'Taking liberties, sucking up, usual thing,' agreed Reginald.

'Quiet now.' Paddy Ever, the director – or Ever Anxious, as he was known – had moved forward to take command. He leaned over the pit and shouted up at the stage.

'Why are we wearing a cloak, darling, in the kitchen?'

Cinderella, Reginald could see, looked confused.

'Wardrobe said it was a cloak for this scene. Suppose I'm cold in this bloody great kitchen, no central heating.'

The musicians smiled among themselves. At the beginning of the day they were ready to respond to any kind of joke, no matter how feeble.

Paddy scratched his head. 'I mean, *would* Cinderella suddenly be in a cloak? *Why* would she be in a cloak, now, but only in a dress in the last scene? Is it viable, is all I'm asking. Is it *rational*?'

Paddy's worries were known to hold up proceedings, sometimes for ages. The musicians flicked their music, rested their instruments. They could be in for a long spell of problem-thrashing before Lewis requested their first chord.

'Don't be daft, Pad: cloak on, amazing quick change in the dark. Stands to reason.'

Paddy's face briefly relaxed. Reginald did not envy him his job. 'Balldress under . . . point taken, darling. But why the sudden lipstick?'

They could hear Cinderella sigh. 'Can't put lipstick on in the dark, can I?'

'Righty-ho, lipstick on. Let's go.'

The Winterstown pantomime was all a very different kettle of fish to the Palladium, Reginald thought, as he did every year.

The rehearsal began. Cinderella and the Fairy Godmother, a dear old thing who had been in panto for years and whose underarms, these days, swung as the wand waved, played the scene too far downstage for Reginald to see anything. He could only just hear Valerie's sweet voice and strange emphasis. 'Oh, god*mother* . . .' He liked such original rendering.

It wasn't till after the mid-morning coffee break that the musicians were required to play the few high notes whose purpose, as Lewis so often explained, was to convey excitement. There was drama with the ponies, as usual: two nasty little Shetlands, hired at great expense from an animal psychiatrist, but who had minds of their own just the same. They refused to stand still, and laid back their ears warning what would happen should they be pressed to act against their will. One of them nipped young Andrew, the coachman. A part-time actor mostly out of work, Andrew proudly admitted he started off at the bottom year after year, but remained convinced that one day his moment would come. Trouble was, as he once confided to Reg, he was so nervous of the ponies, despite their small size, that it was all he could do to keep holding their reins, let alone think himself deeply into the part of the coachman. A lamp fell off the coach as soon as Andrew returned from being bandaged, and then the door wouldn't open. 'Bloody useless wand,' snapped the old godmother, longing for her lunchtime Guinness as the carpenter hammered away at the door.

It was a morning full of laughs – the kind of morning that made up for so much of the aching boredom of the job. And at last Cinderella appeared alone in the spotlight, cloakless, dazzling in a dress of sequins splattered on to net. Reginald still could not see her properly: he would have to wait for her upstage number, *I'm going to the ball*, for that. As it was, the wolf-whistles and laughs from the stagehands – an old tradition at any leading lady's first dress rehearsal – made him uncomfortable. For all its good humour, Reginald did not like the idea of Valerie in all her finery being laughed at.

At the lunch break, Reginald hurried out alone from the pit. He had to break the news to his mother – whose dinner was, thank God, provided by Meals on Wheels today – that there was to be an unscheduled rehearsal this afternoon, due to delays this morning caused by the coach and ponies. Her outrage was predictable. He would have to listen to ten minutes of abuse and insult – 'If you were Sir Thomas blinking Beecham I might understand' – before providing her with a calming glass of brandy and making his escape. Dreading the scene ahead, he barged clumsily round the corner that led to the stage door, and bumped into Valerie herself. She was still in her balldress. The sequins, in the poor winter light, looked asleep.

'Excuse me, I'm so sorry . . .'

'Reg, isn't it?' Cinderella gave him a wonderful smile. Her grasp of every name in the company endeared her to all.

'I have to let my mother know . . .'

'Like the dress? Isn't it gross?' She laughed. 'See you later.'

Reginald spun home, weightless. His mother's fury, the

cold sausage for his lunch, the smell of the kitchen, the jibes at his general uselessness, meant nothing to him. Impervious to everything but the extraordinary thumping of his heart, inspired by Cinderella's smile, he was in and out of the house with astonishing speed. As he hurried back up the garden path, almost enjoying his mother's wailing in his ears, Reginald knew he was in love with Cinderella, and was to spend the afternoon playing for her alone while she danced above him at the ball.

In the next two weeks of rehearsal, Reginald did not run into Valerie backstage again. But in his new state of love he was quite happy to be patient, to hear her sweet voice above him, hear the tapping of her feet, and to catch the occasional glimpse of her when she was upstage. Her prancing little body and enchanting smile were particularly appealing in her ragged dress, though he saw her best at the ball: the choreographer had naturally arranged for the prince to waltz with his Cinderella as far upstage as possible. Reginald, putting his soul into every note of the banal waltz, followed her steps as Bev swung her about. They gazed into each other's eyes, the woman and the girl, acting the kind of happiness which was so convincing it caused Reginald a jealous stab. Fact was, they were much better actors than he had ever given them credit for. The audience would believe this was Prince Charming – not Bev the part-time optician's model – in love with Cinderella, not Valerie who, Reginald knew, sometimes sang in a pub to make ends meet.

He longed for an event that he knew would never happen: waltzing *himself* with Cinderella in some posh hotel ballroom with chandeliers, far from Winterstown. Then on the balcony of their suite, the moonlight and roses bit: he would play a little tune – one of his own compositions, maybe, while she sipped champagne. Next, he would kiss her. So hard she could no longer smile. After that . . . but there his fantasies stalled. He could only imagine a paling dawn sky.

None of that would ever happen. It was some consolation, watching her, to know that at least *this* was all make-believe. What Reginald could not have borne would have been Val (she had become Val in his mind) dancing, in real life, with another man. He closed his eyes as he pulled the final note from his violin. He longed.

At the first performance of *Cinderella*, as always, there was a full house. The audience, mostly pensioners and school-children, loved it. Val, taking many bows, had never looked so appealing. She and Prince Charming held hands and smiled copiously at each other. Reginald would have liked to have gone round to her dressing-room and joined the crowd of admirers he presumed would be there, tell her she was wonderful. As it was, he had to hurry. His mother would be furious at his lateness caused by the prolonged applause.

Once again, he ran into Valerie, surprisingly, in the passage that led to the dressing-rooms. She was still in her balldress, an old cardigan slung around her shoulders.

'Good first house, wasn't it?'

Reginald nodded. The compliments rose, then withered in his throat.

'Bev and I are just off for a hamburger. See you.'

She was gone.

On his way home, Reginald decided what to do – for now, he believed, he should waste no more time, act fast. He would send her flowers. Huge great bunch in cellophane, small card in the envelope saying *From a secret admirer*. The thought of this plan went some way to dispelling his fury with himself for not speaking to her. She must think him a useless old man. But time would change all that. Plans beginning to crowd his head, he opened the front door.

'Is that you, Reg?' His mother's shriek was more than usually annoyed.

Protected from her by his inner strategies, Reginald went calmly to deal with her cocoa, the wearying process of putting her to bed, and all the arrows of her fury.

Reginald dreamed that night of himself and Cinderella at a princely ball, but he never sent the flowers. He managed to leave early enough, next morning, to get to the florist before rehearsals for a concert. But he was so confused by the scents and colours and prices, he left without buying. He'd had in mind pure white lilies, or cream old-fashioned roses mixed with cornflowers – the kind of thing his father had been so proud of in his border. The florist seemed to have only crude red or rust flowers on stiff stems, leaves unbending as swords. Nothing worthy of Cinderella.

Then, just as he was coming out of the shop – the assistant's eyes contemptuous on his back – he observed Val and Bev walking down the other side of the High Street. Both wore jeans and anoraks. For a moment it was quite hard to recognise them. They paused, kissed each other on the cheek, and Bev disappeared into Boots. Valerie, turning to continue on her way, saw Reginald. She waved, smiled her glorious smile, arming him for the day against all adversities.

There were plenty of those. At the rehearsal for a concert in the Winterstown Hall, Lewis was at his most waspish and petulant, quibbling with Tom's tone and Reg's high C, and sneering so hard at poor old Jim Reed on the drums it was a wonder the man did not resign on the spot. But as his bow soared through the *Enigma Variations*, transporting him to the English countryside in May, walking in mead-owlands with Cinderella, it came to Reginald that the only way to make any progress with her was to *do* something. Like ask her out for a drink.

At the lunch break that day the other members of the orchestra left for an hour in the pub. Reginald could not be persuaded to join them. He wanted to be on his own: Meals on Wheels was dealing with his mother. There was no reason to move.

He sat, violin across his knees, in the forest of empty chairs on the stage. The music played on in his ears, not disturbing the real silence. Down in the vast hall, chairs were stacked against the walls ready to be regimented for the next concert. A thin rain pattered against high win-dows. The light on the bare walls was dull as old stone, and it was cold. But Reginald spent an undisturbed lunch hour, oblivious of everything around him, walking with Valerie in Herefordshire (a place he had always longed to visit). He was, for once, at peace.

After the performance that night he hurried to the stage

door, and then out into the alleyway at the back of the theatre. It was still raining, a cold hard rain that damply spotted his mackintosh. He stood, eyes on the square light of the glass door, violin case under one arm, heart pumping audibly. Members of the cast and orchestra came out in groups, and singly. Once a show was under way, nobody planned much of a social life after performances. They were all keen to get home.

Almost last, Valerie emerged. She wore a scarf wound high round her neck, but no hat. In the rain, and the light from within, the frizzy mop of her hair glittered like a swarm of fireflies. Behind her, Bev was talking to the porter at the stage door. She wore her imitation leopardskin coat and seemed to be cross about something. Val saw Reg.

'What's up, darling?' she asked.

Reg moved his free hand on to the solid, familiar curves of his violin case.

'I was wondering,' he said, 'if you'd care for a quick drink on your way home?'

He deliberately said quick because there was not much time. He had taken the precaution of making up some story to his mother about having to see the manager, but her credulity would not stretch far. Half an hour's grace, at the most.

Val laughed. It was not the friendly laugh. But perhaps sound was distorted here, out in the rain.

'Why not?' she said. 'Bev and I and some of the others are going down to the Drake. Want to join us?'

Reg paused for a second. Val's idea did not fit in with his plan at all. The last thing he wanted was to be with her in a crowd, perhaps unable to exchange a word. He wanted her to himself, just a small table, somewhere, between them. He wanted her full attention while he told her some of the things that had been piling within for as long as he could remember, and had never been spoken. His violin had been the sole recipient of his feelings, the music his only consolation. But man cannot live by music alone, as Tom, who had many an eager woman on his arm, so often said.

'I don't think I will, thanks. My mother . . .'

'Very well. Another time.' Val was not interested. But then something of the approaching Christmas spirit, Reginald supposed it was, entered her funny little head. She decided to be kind. 'But tell you what: tomorrow after the matinee? Bev's going to the dentist so we can't go over to her mum as per usual. We could have a coffee.'

'A coffee?'

A kaleidoscope of difficulties swooped through Reg's brain. More excuses to his mother would have to be thought up, and where would be a suitable place to go?

'Very well,' he said.

'Meet you here after the show, then. Bev!'

Bev hurried out, glanced at Reg. Val was all smiles.

'Blimey, what a night.' Bev snapped up an umbrella, put her arm round Val, drawing her beneath it. 'Cheers, Reg,' Bev said, and Reginald watched Val slip her arm into the crook of the nylon leopardskin one.

They moved away, in step, huddled snugly under the umbrella, confident of its shelter, like those people in the advertisement for a life insurance company. Reginald waited till they were out of sight. Then, hugging his violin case, he turned into the full blast of the rain, in the direction of home.

Reginald and Val sat at a small table in the window of the Wimpy Bar - nearest eating place to the theatre. Reginald had suggested they go to the tearooms further down the High Street, altogether a more comfortable place, but Val had insisted she fancied chips in the Wimpy.

Two cups of thin coffee sat between them. Val covered her chips with spurts of ketchup from a plastic tomato. Reginald kept one hand on his violin case, propped up beside him. His head was empty from lack of sleep. He was drained, exhausted, by his imaginings. He didn't know where to begin. Ten minutes of their half-hour had passed, and all he had done was to make a disparaging remark about Lewis Crone. Val had disagreed. She said far as she was concerned he was a good sport.

'It must be boring down in the pit,' she said eventually, 'not seeing anything.'

'You can see enough. I get a good view of you dancing in the ball scene.'

'That!' Val laughed, more friendly than last night. 'See Bev treading on my toes? She's a horrible dancer.'

She laid one hand flat on the Formica tabletop, examined her nails with great interest as she slightly lifted each finger in turn. Reginald wanted to cover her hand with his.

'You're a lovely dancer, though,' he said.

Val gave him a teasing look. 'Reg! Haven't you got a wife, a woman? Someone? You always look so down in the dumps.'

'There's my mother to be looked after.' Reg suppressed a sigh and tapped his violin case. 'There's my music. I'm all right, just not one of life's jokers.'

'No.'

The speech Reg had rehearsed most of the night, inspired by Bach under the bedclothes, welled. It was now or never, he thought.

'But I'd like to get to know you – nothing . . . out of line. Cup of tea sometimes. Talk. You know. I haven't much of a life socially. What with my mother. Drink with Tom, Saturdays. End of a concert drink with the boys. Not occasions to talk . . .'

Reg petered out, aware he had lost the thread of his message. The rubbish he was talking sounded close to self-pity. He didn't want Val's pity: last thing he wanted. And she had stopped picking at her chips. She pushed her empty cup away, stiff-handed. Gave a tight little smile, as if she decided she must get through this little scene as graciously as possible, but it was boring.

'Poor old Reg. Well, it's fine by me if we have another coffee some time. Though I'm leaving Winterstown, March. Doing three months in Manchester, an Agatha Christie.'

Reginald's heart contracted. He would have to think about that later: the bleakness of the spring.

'Anyway,' she smiled, nicely this time, 'you must be fifteen years older than me, Reg.'

'Probably.'

It was dark outside now. The pair of them made awkward shapes reflected in the plate-glass window. Madness seized Reg so fast he was unable to control it, to reason with himself.

'But I'm over the moon about you, see. Nothing bothersome, mind. Just, watching you dancing away, Cinderella in her ballgown, I fancied your pretty smile was for me. Daft, I know.' He saw her look of alarm, tried to slow himself. 'All I want is to talk to you, don't I? To tell you things, give you a good time, spend my savings on you. I've a fair bit put on one side – nothing to spend my wages on all these years. What do you think, Val? Would you let me, sometimes?'

Val gave a small laugh, perturbed. 'I don't want anything like that, nice though you are.'

'No. Well. I didn't rate my chances high.'

'It's not that I'd mind a chat from time to time. But Bev wouldn't like it. There'd be trouble. I've had enough trouble.'

'Trouble with Bev?'

'Bev's my friend.'

'I know Bev's your friend. But she can't order your life about. A woman.'

Val sighed. 'Have to be going,' she said. 'Meeting her at six.'

'Meeting Bev? What's she got, this Bev?'

In his confusion, Reg could not be sure of anything. But for a moment – so short he might have imagined it – he thought Val looked scared.

'A nasty temper if things don't go her way.'

'You shouldn't put up with her. I mean, do you *like* her?' Later, Reg reflected, his boldness may have been impertinent.

Val shrugged. 'Thanks for the coffee 'n' chips.' She stood up, swirling the scarf round her neck.

'Cinderella,' said Reg. 'Cinderella.'

She bent briefly towards him. He could smell her breath: ketchup, chips, coffee. She patted his shoulder.

'Chin up, Reg.'

'I want you to know' – her hand fled from his shoulder – 'that every performance it's you I'm playing for, Val, down there, all that rubbishy music. One day I could play you Brahms, on a beach somewhere, tide coming in, never go back to the orchestra. They'll never make me first violin is what I'm afraid of, not even when Tom goes. You could, you could come with—'

Val turned from his jibbering, impatient. Reg could tell from her eyes she thought he was a silly old fool, letting go.

'What you must remember is this, Reg.' Her voice was harsh as flint now, cutting the quick of him. 'You're a nice guy, but I'm another kind of Cinderella.'

She was gone. Striding through the purplish light, the ketchup tables, the bleak landscape of Formica and burgers. Reginald remained standing, clutching his violin case, peering through the window. In the late-night shopping crowds he thought he glimpsed a leopardskin coat, but of Val he could see nothing.

That night he kept his eyes on the music, did not look up to see Cinderella in her balldress dancing with Bev the prince. Reg had always known she was not for him, any more than was the position of first violin. But who was she for? What did she mean, another kind of Cinderella?

After the performance he hurried off to avoid an accidental meeting. It was a night full of ironic stars. Just twenty-four hours ago, in the rain, she had given him some hope. He didn't know why he bothered with hope, anymore.

'Is that you, Reg?' Furious voice. Usual thing.

Reg made his way slowly across the small, stuffy hall and into the front room. He opened the door, surveyed the familiar picture of the monstrous old woman who was his mother: the mother who had messed up his entire life. Plumped up with indignation, she sat upright in her chair, accusation flaring across her purple cheeks, obscene legs swinging. If it hadn't been for his binding duty to her, things would have been different. If he had been a worse son he would have had a better chance.

'What kept you then? Dancing with Cinderella?'

She gave a sneering laugh, thumping one swollen hand into the soft mess of crochet on her knee. Reginald swung his violin case above his head, and moved towards her in silence before they both screamed.

*D*ressing *U*p

'Please, just one more chance,' cooed Prunella in her most persuasive voice. 'Just lunch and the afternoon.'

There was a long silence while her daughter Audrey, on the other end of the line, struggled to weigh up the pros and cons of her mother's request.

Prunella, although dreading this call, was fed up with watching time flood by with no sight of her grandchildren. It was over two months, now, since the unfortunate incident. Surely enough time for anyone to find forgiveness. But Audrey had never been rich in charity. Even as a small child she had shown signs of her father's hardness. She was vigorous in her condemnation, ungenerous in her understanding. Prunella had always been a dutiful mother, and hoped she always would be. But she couldn't like Audrey.

And how beastly she had been about the incident. A very minor mishap: no ill effects on the children. They had had *fun*, as they always did have when they came to their grandmother. More than they had at home, for the most part. It wasn't Prunella's fault Audrey had been held up in traffic, so arrived late to collect them on that particular day. Well, by six, half an hour later than her usual time for the first one, Prunella was exhausted, in need of something. She must have had two gins and tonics before Audrey arrived. Having started late, perhaps she had drunk them faster than usual. What with one thing and another, on the way down the path to Audrey's car she had stumbled, cut her knee, felt dizzy. There had been quite a palaver, Audrey pulling her up, grumbling away, telling the children to buzz off and find a plaster. 'You're irresponsible, Mother,' she had hissed when the children, all sympathy for their grandmother, had run off. 'How do you expect me to feel about leaving them with someone who *drinks*? Anything could happen. I shan't let them come again.'

Prunella hadn't felt like arguing. She had sat on a kitchen chair, one stocking an ignominious roll beneath her knee, watching Audrey savagely dab the bloody patch. The children hugged her goodbye, said they hoped they would see her soon. She had given them a box of chocolates, which afforded Audrey the opportunity for a familiar lecture on children's teeth before hurrying them away. Prunella hadn't seen them since then. Audrey was carrying out her threat. This was her punishment. Drink: and no grandchildren. Deprivation of the two people who gave her most pleasure on earth, these days. She was a callous monster, Audrey. How could she have given birth to one of so little compassion?

But this silly feud had gone on long enough, Prunella thought, at dawn the autumn day of the call she eventually forced herself to make. She must put an end to it. She must swallow pride and anger, apologise, make promises not to touch a drop before the children arrived or while they were there: promise anything. She must compromise herself in a disgraceful way. But any form of humiliation was worth it to see the grandchildren.

At eleven o'clock she drank two cups of coffee without their usual addition of brandy. This daily booster, she had found, gave the necessary strength for the rest of the day. Unfortunately, Audrey's antennae were so acute she seemed able to tell if her mother had put so much as a dash of sherry in her trifle, just by her voice over the telephone. So this morning, wanting to take no risks, Prunella had denied herself fortification. Without it she was feeling very shaky. The receiver of the telephone danced at her ear. Sweat frosted the back of her neck. Her heart was leaping like a young lamb.

'One more chance, then,' said Audrey at last, in her tight little voice. 'You know the conditions.'

'I know the conditions. Of course I—'

'Just lunch and the afternoon. I'll drop them at twelve. And no chocolates either, please.'

'Poor mites! Very well, no chocolates. I've missed them so much. They must wonder why they haven't been for so long.'

'They haven't said anything.'

Prunella knew Audrey was lying. She was able to detect her daughter's lies on the telephone every bit as distinctly as Audrey could detect her own small indulgence of alcohol. But this morning she didn't care. The main thing was she had won the battle. The horrible waiting, the isolation, was over. She would see the children in just two days. Dear George, gallant beyond his years: Anna of the laughing eyes. Prunella poured herself a third cup of coffee, laced it with a fierce shot of brandy.

She was determined to take no risks. After breakfast on

31

the day of the children's visit, she put the bottle of brandy in the dining-room cupboard – a cold, deserted room she scarcely visited – and locked it. She put the key in the pocket of her apron, hoping she would forget where it was. Back in the warmth of the kitchen she placed a tea cosy over the bottle of gin. The smile of its white label stretching across its elegant green shoulders was the temptation evenings, afternoons, that she could not resist So long as it was hidden, she would be quite safe.

The hours passed so fast in busy preparation of the children's food that Prunella did not stop for her usual cup of coffee, let alone brandy. At twelve, everything ready, the table laid, Ribena poured, she remembered this and smiled to herself. Sometimes, it was so easy. When you were happy, there was no need for a booster. Maybe she'd leave the brandy in the cupboard. Not touch it tomorrow, either. Make a real effort. Sling out the grinning gin. *Reform*, as Audrey would say. Though what would Audrey know about the near-impossibility of such a thing?

The bell rang on the dot of twelve-thirty. Audrey was always punctual, and superior with it. She gave a hurried smile, trying to disguise the twitching of her nostrils, the mean detection of drink on her mother's breath. Hoping to catch me out, the bitch, thought Prunella. But it didn't matter. With George and Anna wriggling under each arm, she felt bold, strong.

'Do I pass the breath test?'

'Don't be stupid, Mother. I'll be back at five.'

Once Audrey had gone the children burst from strait-jackets of polite demeanour – always worn in the shadow of their mother – and hugged their grandmother so hard she was almost knocked over. She managed to brush aside any answers to their questions about why they had not seen her for so long with the promise of small presents awaiting them in the kitchen. She produced shiny black pencils with their names engraved in gold, with notebooks to match – 'For your secret thoughts,' she said. The children laughed. They were always delighted by the quaintness of their grandmother's presents, so carefully chosen. At home, they were rich in computer games, Walkmans, miniature televisions – quick, easy, expensive presents which could be bought with no trouble. Spoiled in this respect, they still appreciated real worth: their grandmother's presents were of especial value.

Prunella's kitchen, where she spent most of her time, blazed with signals of her life. Old photographs, lists, theatre posters, half-finished pieces of tapestry were either stuck to the walls or piled on the floor or chairs. It was not uncommon to find grated carrot in a pair of satin evening shoes that had lodged by the stove for the past twenty years, or a rusty trinket in the fruit bowl. The children, accustomed to the white Formica sterility of their own kitchen at home, loved the room. It bulged with memories of happy afternoons since their earliest childhood, and was always full of the warm expectation of exciting things to come. Occasionally they would venture into the large, cold, unused rooms of the house, deserted since their grandfather had died. But they thought of them as sad, dead rooms, that made shivers run down their backs, and would quickly hurry back to the life of the kitchen.

As usual, they ate hungrily of their grandmother's food, made promises not to tell about the chocolate pudding. They listened enchanted as she told stories about her intriguing past, which had been a very glamorous time, and indeed she had been very famous. A dancer, a singer, a bit of both – and only twenty years ago some television company had come and persuaded her to talk about her past: they had seen the recording over and over again. She was a star, their grandmother, they could tell from the many photographs of a beautiful face that smiled from the mists of the old photographs on the walls. And even today she was a star, bright red hair – the children didn't believe it when their mother said it was a wig – long gipsy earrings, scarlet nails, silver eye-shadow. But for the wrinkles, she could be mistaken for a rock star, they thought. And underneath her apron she wore velvet dresses of crimson or purple or sapphire that flashed a patchwork of light, and she smelt of face powder from a bygone age.

'And what shall we do today?' she was saying. 'How best shall we pass the afternoon, little ones?'

'Dressing up,' they said.

'I thought so,' said Prunella. Of all the old-fashioned activities she thought up for them, dressing up was the favourite. 'I brought down some new things from the attic.'

In a trice they had leapt upon the huge cardboard box waiting under the window. (It had taken three whiskies, last night, to give Prunella the strength to drag it down from the attic.)

'How did you get this down all by yourself, Gran?'

'Easily!'

'You're brilliant, Gran,' said Anna.

Prunella, dumping dirty plates into the sink to be washed at some future time she had no wish to think about, beamed. She listened to the small cries of amazement and amusement as the children plucked pantomime clothes from the box. They would pull something on, then, more strongly attracted by something else, pull it off before it was in place.

The dishes cleared, Prunella sat at the table giving advice and encouragement. She panted a little, felt a little light-headed. Well, the children's visits were dizzy times, stirring up the stale old quietness till the kitchen became a place she could hardly recognise. Besides, she had worked so hard this morning, never a moment off her feet.

What she wanted was a drink.

The children were ready at last. George was a small laughing cavalier, ostrich feather swooping from his velvet cap right under his chin; Anna was a shepherdess with a laced bodice and yellow silk stockings.

'Wonderful!' Prunella clapped her hands. 'You look real professionals.' This, they knew, was her highest compliment: she had been the most professional professional in her time. 'Now for acting.'

'Not without you, Gran.'

'What, me? Dress up too?'

This moment of mock surprise was a small charade enjoyed every visit. Prunella would feign reluctance, then find herself persuaded.

'Well,' she would say, as she did now, 'if that's what you

want . . .' And they would shower her with myriad things to choose from till she, too, had become a character, a star from some world-famous theatrical show.

Prunella stood up. Knees shaky. She fended off the gust of scarves and jackets they threw at her.

'Just a moment, darlings. Gran just needs a . . . to keep her going. Put on some music, George, why not? Let's begin with our old *Blackbird* to put us in the mood.' She opened the fridge, took out the bottle of white wine. She poured herself a tumbler.

George, child of the technological age, always had some trouble with the workings of the maplewood box his grandmother called the radiogram. But eventually he persuaded the old table to spin the 78 record – *Bye Bye, Blackbird*. They had known all the words for years.

'When somebody says to me
Sugar sweet, so is she
Bye bye, blackbird . . .'

Within moments, Prunella found herself pumping the old power into the song. The once-famous voice trembled poignantly on every note, drowning the thinner voices of the children. She drank a second glass, picked up her skirts, pointed a velvet shoe with a diamanté buckle.

'Now, off we go. Follow the silly old bat, won't you? *Bye, bye, blackbird . . .*'

'You're not a silly old bat, Gran.'

The children knew the rules: copy every movement precisely. This afternoon Prunella was full of invention. They skipped around the table waving their arms as if carrying invisible boughs. They grabbed apples from the bowl and threw them high. They flicked their fingers under a running tap at the sink. They – and this was their favourite part – climbed up a chair on to the table, creaking the old pine top as they twirled between bowls of hyacinths – and then leapt down the other side. Those brief moments high on the table felt like being on a stage.

'Oh, happy chorus line, darlings,' Prunella sang. She downed a third quick glass. 'Up we go again, why not?'

This time, on the table top, she did a few steps of the can-can. Amazed by their grandmother's high kicks, the children gave up trying to copy her. They watched, entranced.

'Not the right music, of course, but I can still kick a leg, can't I? Let's see if I can't find a can-can record.'

Prunella, jumping ambitiously back down on to a chair, missed her footing. There was a crack, a thud and a dignified whimper, all muffled by the music as she flung one fat arm dramatically behind her.

'Gran? – Quick, George,' shouted Anna.

George slithered off the table, laughing. He bent over Prunella on the floor.

'Are you doing your dying scene, Gran?'

Anna prodded a vast velvet hip, its lights twinkling less brightly in the shadow of the table. She could see, so close to Prunella's eyelids, the smudges of silvery blue were thick and uneven. The lids looked like wrinkled blue worms lying side by side. When her eyes were open, you didn't notice this. Anna wished they would open now. The record slurred to the end. Now the only sound was the running tap.

'You can get up now, Gran,' she said.

'Think she's dead?' asked George.

'I suppose I'd better feel her heart.' Anna was top in biology at school. She ran a reluctant finger over the left velvet breast, feeling the warmth but no distinctive heart-beat.

'There's stuff coming out of her mouth,' observed George, 'and isn't she a funny colour? Maybe she's unconscious.'

'I'll ring for an ambulance.' Anna's coolness in a crisis had been rewarded by making her a prefect. All the same, the telephone jittered in her hand.

'Better not say she's dead,' said George, 'or they won't hurry.'

One of the ambulancemen removed the scarlet boa from Prunella's neck and quickly plunged down, locking his mouth on to hers.

'Kiss of life,' Anna explained to George.

'Wouldn't fancy that,' George giggled. The ambulance-man sat back on his heels, frowning. 'You've got lipstick all over you.'

'Pipe down, young chappie. What about you two?'

'Our mother will be here any minute,' said Anna.

'That's good, because we'd best get a move on.' He was helping the second man to attach a drip to Prunella's arm, still stiff in its last flourish.

It was a struggle to lift her on to the stretcher. One of her shoes fell off. The boa left scarlet feathers on the ambulancemen's uniforms. George deplored the sight of his grandmother's knee, suddenly revealed, that only moments ago had been so impressive in its kicks.

'Poor old Gran,' said Anna. She hated the sight of the shock of copper hair tipped sideways, proving her mother was right about a wig. She hoped George would not notice.

'If she's not dead, then it's her best ever dying Juliet.' Tears of admiration ran quietly down George's cheeks.

Audrey, hurrying punctually down the path, found her way impeded by the ambulancemen and stretcher. In the second she paused, she saw the multi-coloured mound of her mother, clown-white face smudged with blue eyebrows, powdery blobs of salmon pink ironic on the old cheeks. She screamed.

From the front door the children watched her livid journey.

'Cool it, Mum. Gran had a fall.' Anna herself felt a strange calm.

Audrey swivelled round at the slamming of the ambulance doors.

'You *idiots*! Of all the stupid . . . Quick, we must follow her.' She ripped off George's hat and threw it nastily to the ground. 'What *happened*?' George retrieved his hat. He had no time to answer before Audrey ran into the kitchen, saw the empty bottle, the up-turned chair. Again the children watched her from the door.

'Christ! I can't believe it. Never, ever again . . .' she shouted, exploding eyes glassy with tears.

Anna hitched up her skirt with pitiless hands.

'No use threatening us,' she said. 'Gran may be dead.'

'On the other hand,' said George, 'it may just be one of her best dying scenes.'

He knew about the sweetness of revenge from his history books, and the power it could engender. With a solemn look he replaced his feathered hat, tilting it in just the way his grandmother had assured him, light years ago, was appropriate for a laughing cavalier.

The Day
of the QE2

Nothing very much ever happens in Ballymorning, a small town of little significance on the Irish coast. While the folk who live there are proud of its tranquillity, they do sometimes wish that a quiver of excitement would bestir the peace that lies flat, heavy, stifling, over its uncrowded streets and shops of unfashionable gentility. Even the pubs afford little gaiety, except on the occasions of a wedding party or a funeral wake.

The young of Ballymorning usually leave for Dublin or Cork as soon as they are able, there being no work and no temptations to keep them at home. If they feel any nostalgia for the town of their birth when they have gone, this is not reflected in the number of occasions they visit their homes. Once departed from Ballymorning, resigned parents know, there is little likelihood of their offspring returning. There is a familiar pattern, discussed by many a mother who has done her best, of contact with grown-up children becoming more infrequent. It is the penalty, perhaps, for such peace and quiet.

Some years ago, a few of Ireland's tourists began to discover the limited attractions of Ballymorning. The view from its harbour is the thing they like best. You can see them standing there in little groups, identifiable by their anoraks the colours of nursery rhymes, polystyrene beakers of coffee in hand, gazing out beyond the curve of the giant harbour wall, allowing their gaze to follow the North Sea to the horizon. Sometimes they sit on the coils of tarred rope. Eyes strained by the abstract contemplation of the sea, which tells them nothing, they seek relief in the seagulls bouncing in the air above them, their orchestrated shrieks making contemporary music that shreds all contemplation. They point their cameras this way and that, these tourists whose delight is to notch up places on film, and go on to somewhere better supplied with amusement.

The older inhabitants of Ballymorning do what they can to take advantage of this new, albeit thin trade. Irene O'Connor, in the Post Office and General Stores, has initiated a sideline in homemade soda bread and scones. She's up half the night baking, but the profit, in the summer season, is worth her effort. Her neighbour Jack Riley, formerly a tinker, applied himself to the renovating of his old pony trap. He spent three months polishing, painting, mending, oiling. Then he clipped his old piebald cob, long since retired from the shafts, and advertised rides in the trap down to the harbour and back. This proved popular with visitors longing to be free of their children for quarter of an hour. One look at Jack and his quaint transport, and trust reared its cautious head. There was no doubt the children would be in safe hands. And they were. Jack made them laugh with stories of his past life on the road. Word of this entertainment travelled. Takings are now good. The pony cart rides cause a seasonal ripple in Jack's retirement. The benefits of initiative have come to him just in time to enliven his old age, and he is able to offer more copious rounds of Guinness in the pub. He feels quite proud.

Tom Deary, retired teacher and part-time barber, is another of Ballymorning's inhabitants to have been inspired by the thought of making profit from the tourists. Tom is a character who commands universal respect in the town: so kindly and mild a man there never was. He is said to have come from some minor aristocratic family, about which he is modestly vague. This belief was strengthened in 1952, when an uncle bequeathed to Tom his almost new Armstrong-Siddeley. A suitable garage was built for the wondrous car, which had only travelled 130 miles in its five years of life. Tom, perhaps inheriting a reservation about mileage in his genes, has only added some eighty-four miles to that number in the last forty-five years. Those miles were most reluctantly agreed to: on one occasion he allowed the Armstrong-Siddeley to be used as a wedding car for his niece Sheila, who then took the further liberty of asking Tom to drive herself and her husband to their honeymoon hotel some way to the south. This caused Tom many traumas concerning the lodging of confetti on the carpeted floor, and in the difficult places between the leather seats. The second occasion for the car's outing was a charitable cause. A neighbour's daughter, crippled by an accident, requested a trip in a fairy-coach for a birthday treat. Her desperate mother reckoned Tom's car was the nearest Ballymorning could get to the desired coach, and set about her persuading. Tom found himself in a morally weak position. He could hardly say no to such a request, and wondered at the reluctance of his heart. He agreed with a smile which he hoped would disguise his feelings. And once they were on the road, mother and daughter on the back seat full of praises for his careful driving, his amorphous fears vanished. He had taken the precaution of covering the seat (against what, he could not say, even to himself) with sheets of plastic and several rugs, and in the very slow covering of seven miles, much to Tom's relief, nothing untoward happened.

No: to Tom Deary transport was not the point of the Armstrong-Siddeley. So grand a car, for a start, was not for the modest likes of him. To drive about in a machine of gleaming green paint and sparkling chrome would have been quite out of keeping with his character. It would have looked like pride. It would also have alienated him from his friends who owned lesser cars, or those who could only rely on public transport. To Tom, the car was simply a trophy: a symbol of the best of British craftsmanship, a sample from the days when cars *were* cars, beautifully hand-finished things which, in return for love and care and attention, would remain in pristine condition for more than a century.

Tom, who had once loved but never married, spent all his spare time on the upkeep of his inherited car. Three evenings a week he polished, vacuumed, treated the owl-eyed headlights to doses of Windowlene wiped carefully off with the most expensive chamois leather. Regularly he sent off to Dublin for supplies of superior beeswax polish with which to maintain the gleam of the walnut dashboard, with its irregular pattern of small round windows set in silver frames. Behind these, very simple dials remained unmoving, until the occasional moments when Tom turned the key and pressed the starter button, and the small arrows jumped to life telling him what he knew, but liked to have confirmed: petrol tank full, oil fine. He kept the smart little clock, also inlaid into the walnut, wound. When, at the end of his work, he would sit in the driver's seat, relishing the smell of the fat leather seats the colour of Jersey cows, the comforting silence was scarcely chipped by the discreet tick of this gallant little clock. Garage doors open wide, sun beating on to the dazzling bonnet, stuffy warmth making him drowsy in his stationary Armstrong-Siddeley – this, for Tom Deary, was happiness.

In all probability, nothing would ever have changed his routine had there not been a sudden crisis in the garage roof. A particularly hard wind caused it to let in rain in several places – a tacky construction, the garage, for all its expense, and now presenting real danger to the well-being of the car. Tom lived on a meagre teacher's pension – there was not much barbering these days, and the old wisps of hair he still tidied up were always 'on the house'. So how could he pay for repairs to the garage roof? Tom put the matter to Jack Riley, who in a conspiratorial whisper made mention of the fact that he, Jack, was doing very nicely out of his little business with the pony cart. Tom then recalled that his great-niece, Sheila's daughter, imprisoned in a loveless marriage, had mentioned she was doing well from her own sideline, selling postcards down by the harbour. The tourists were obviously the answer to his prayer, Tom thought. He walked slowly into the night, a sharp fishwind coming up from the sea, to reflect upon how he himself could take advantage of them.

There was a struggle in his soul all night long, for Tom knew that the single thing he had to offer was the Armstrong-Siddeley. The problem was, the very thought of strangers riding in his car, however exorbitant the fare, cast his spirits so low he could feel a physical sawing in his breast bone, and in all his sobriety he felt the weak dizziness of a drunk man. Why, strangers with no appreciation of fine things would be up to all manner of tricks. They would stuff sweet papers down the arms, spill drinks on the carpet, blot out the sweet smell of the leather upholstery with their own crude scents of sweat and cheap aftershave. Tom could not bear to contemplate such things. Besides, driving them along the lanes he would be so worried about the possible lapses in behaviour that his power of concentration would be at serious risk. He might land them all in a ditch, destroying the car completely. No, there would have to be another way.

It came to him early in the morning: an idea so simple, so watertight, he wondered it had not occurred to him sooner. It was this: on fine days (business would be closed should rain threaten), he would ease the car into the road outside his house and allow any passing visitor to sit in it, for anything up to half an hour, for a small fee. Just to *sit*, mind. Never in the driver's seat, and with the doors open, to make sure any alien smells could not be harboured. Tom himself would pace round the vehicle, keeping a beady eye while he regaled his customers with stories of the car's history. Here, he acknowledged, as the car had led a somewhat dull life mostly in the garage, he would be forced to use his teacher's imagination, and work on a few embellishments.

Should there be any sign of untoward action, such as a sticky sweet being unwrapped, the offender would be politely requested to get out of the car at once.

This, it seemed to Tom, was the perfect solution. Tourists would be only too willing, surely, to pay for such an experience. Though it might lack the predictable excitement of a big dipper, or the charm of listening to Jack Riley's pony's hooves making their olden-days clip-clop on the cobbled streets as they sat in the uncomfortable seats of his cart, this would be something quite different, unimagined. Luxury! What Tom could advertise, in the modern jargon he so despised, but appreciated its uses, was *quality experience*. For how many people had ever seen so beautiful a car as the Armstrong-Siddeley? Let alone sat in one? Oh yes, he was on to a winner. The garage would surely be paid for within weeks.

Tom set about composing his advertisement, which he was to put in the window of the General Stores. He wrote in a fine copperplate hand, but the wording proved difficult. He was not a natural slogan man. Cutting down his description of the Armstrong-Siddeley's attractions to a few compelling words he found very hard. It took some dozen attempts before he was satisfied with the finished advertisement. Meantime, he cleaned the car with extra vigour, and decided on the part of road on which he judged the car would appear to greatest advantage.

Early in the New Year, the first tourists were observed discovering the unusually quiet spot of Ballymorning. The time had come for Tom to launch his business. One morning he opened the garage doors, intent on taking out the car. But somehow he found himself distracted, polishing the back number plate and oiling the ignition key which swung from a tag of real pigskin – the sort of thing not provided by car manufacturers today. On several other occasions, he made serious attempts to begin. It was only a matter of starting the engine, he told himself. But he never quite managed to get the car into the road and, as the weeks, growing warmer, passed by, the Armstrong-Siddeley remained undisturbed in the garage.

One morning in early spring, Tom, like many of the folk of Ballymorning, heard an announcement on the local radio. It seemed that the QE2, on a journey across the Atlantic, was forced to stop, for unspecified technical reasons, just outside Ballymorning's harbour. There it would be anchored, at midday, for some hours. Possibly even the night.

The announcer went on to say that the Mayor of Ballymorning, Clive O'Farell, had lost no time in seizing this opportunity for the people of his town to enjoy the kind of excursion they had never previously imagined. He had arranged for several fishing boats, in return for a small fee, to ferry anyone willing out to the great ship. There, they would be afforded a tour of its amazing decks and staterooms, and given a free cup of tea and plate of luxury cakes (as they were described) before returning home.

Glory be, said Tom Deary to himself, hand shaking badly over his softly boiled egg. How the devil did Clive O'Farell swing that one? Had he simply rung the Captain of the QE2 and put to him the suggestion, claiming it would be a good PR move for Cunard? Tom laughed out loud at the thought. Trust Clive: he'd always been a wily operator. He and Tom had been at school together, sat side by side in class one year. Clive, with his shocking red hair and endearing smile, had been the perpetrator of numerous tricks on teachers. His powerful innocence was always convincing. He was never caught. Tom always knew Clive would go far, and he had certainly accomplished the business with this clever move. The people of Ballymorning would be indebted to him forever – for here, at last, in most unexpected form, was the excitement they had been waiting for, needing, for so long.

Tom hurried off to ring some of his friends, find out how the thinking was going round the town. Even as he picked up the telephone, he knew that his own desire to board the QE2 would have to be sacrificed. Because now, faced with real impetus, crowds drawn to Ballymorning from miles around, he could no longer put off the evil hour. To him, the arrival of the ship was a sign from the Almighty. 'Get up off your backside, Tom Deary,' he could swear he could hear the good Lord saying. And he would. Today would be the launching of the Armstrong-Siddeley. A treat the tourists could never have envisaged. So long as they could find the way to his house (explained at some length at the bottom of his advertisement), Tom had no doubt in his mind that they would find it every bit as rewarding an experience as trudging the long decks of the QE2, and gorging themselves on free cakes.

Others in the town, Tom soon learned, were of his opinion: it would be foolish indeed to waste all the opportunities within reach on this very special day. They had all heard the news at 8 a.m. and again at nine (Tom, polishing the bumpers by then, had missed the repeat). They were all hurrying to prepare for the on-rush of visitors, the like of which they might never see again. Such general astonishment and such delighted shock had not been felt in Ballymorning for as long as anyone could remember.

In the centre of the town it was evident that the radio announcement had caused a considerable flutter. Tom quickly made his way to the General Stores to make sure his advertisement had not been removed from its prominent position in the window. He was pleased to find it still propped between a pyramid of homemade chutney and a basket of early Easter eggs: he was paying 50p a week for the exclusive position. Outside the two pubs, plastic chairs and tables were being dragged on to the pavement by owners who would normally scorn any such niceties. Fruit and vegetables were hastily being arranged in boxes outside the General Stores, a gesture not normally risked due to the changeable nature of the weather. Polly Shaunnessy, in the tobacconist, had come up with the idea of a special offer on dozens of iced lollies she had mistakenly over-ordered some months ago. She had carefully chalked the announcement on her old school slate. In the rush to sell wares, any old wares, several housewives not known for their hospitality now put notices for *Teas* on the front windows and were, Tom presumed with a smile, hastily baking behind their net curtains.

He decided to take a quick look at the harbour, see what was happening down there. After that, he would have to return home, drive the car into the street and be on duty for the rest of the day. In his mind, he saw dozens of visitors, those who preferred the idea of the Armstrong-Siddeley to the QE2, impatiently awaiting their turn to experience its magnificent seats. He might, he felt, have to be quite strict with the visitors: put on his schoolmaster's authoritative voice, insist they wait their turn in orderly fashion.

Five minutes later, he was amazed to see that, already, an unusual amount of cars were parked. Judging from their number plates, they had come from as far afield as Belfast and Cork – why, some of them must have heard the news at six o'clock and started driving towards Ballymorning straight away. Many of them kept to their cars, unspeaking as they took in the stretches of sky and sea before them, drinking tea from flasks. Others, collars up against the breeze, paced back and forth, cameras to the ready, their pleasure at being first, getting the good places, quite evident. None of them was yet drawn to either of the ice-cream vans – there had plainly been an earlier race for the best position. This had been won, by a few yards, by the local lad, Polly Shaunnessy's son Paddy, whose ancient converted van was splashed with wildly spelt promises. *Tuti Gelati! Genuine Italein flavours! Irish-Neapoltan ices!* Paddy's grandmother had come from Naples. His mother had inherited her talent for making ice-cream. Paddy, with his troublesome van that was a familiar sight broken down at the roadside, was one of the few young ones who had used his initiative instead of fleeing to a city, and was making an almost adequate living. Tom was pleased to see Paddy had parked as near as possible to the flight of stone steps that led down from the harbour wall to the fishing boats. He could not have been better placed to catch tourists in the queue to go over to the QE2. Competition, in the shape of a sterile commercial company van plugging 'Softee Ices', had not dared to park so close to the edge of the harbour and the surly-looking salesman within was no match for Paddy Shaunnessy's cheeky charm. It was a grand thing Paddy was the winner in his competition, thought Tom, and bought a chocolate ice to show where his loyalties lay.

'It's a great position you've got yourself here, Paddy . . .' he said. 'You should do well today.'

'I'm hoping so, myself. Are you going over to the big ship?'

Tom shook his head.

'In charge of my own business. Too good an opportunity to miss. It's the car, up there at the house. The Armstrong-Siddeley, all polished fit for the Pope himself. I'm bringing it out for people to sit in. Experience, you know. Should you see anyone fed up with waiting to get over to the QE2, you might oblige me by suggesting there's an alternative treat awaiting them not two streets away.'

'Sure, and I'll do that, Tom. Good luck to you,' said Paddy.

Tom, back to the sea, saw that a great many cars now were crowding into the harbour. There was a traffic jam in the small street that led down to the sea-front. A man was shouting, waving his arms. In the Edwardian houses of dun-coloured stucco and paintwork of long-dead brown, windows were opening, heads appearing. Turning away from this unusual, faintly troubling sight, Tom wandered down the long, narrow arm of the harbour wall that jutted into the sea. He made his way carefully between the nets laid out on the ground to dry. He licked slowly at the superb chocolate ice-cream – there was no commercial firm in the world that could compete with Polly Shaunnessy's ices – and looked over the almost flat grey waters, chipped here and there with sliver shards small as candle flames. There was no sun in the sky, but great braids of light fell vertically from narrow gulfs in the cloud. Tom preferred these subtle colourings of the sea and sky to the more popular blues, sparkling with sun. In the water-colours of Ireland he found a low-key peace. The bright places in travel brochures had never tempted him. The smell of tanning oils made him nauseous. He liked brisk, fresh air. Ice-cream finished, he took a deep breath: smells of salt and fish were plaited into the sea breeze. He had grown up with the constancy of this pungent breeze, and would never desert it to live further inland.

With some reluctance, Tom Deary broke his reflections to turn for home. In truth, he would have liked to stay where he was, eyes fixed on the horizon until the QE2, no more than a white speck the size of a distant gull, cut its way through the distant greys. He would have liked, with the others, to have sailed over to her on one of the rank fishing boats, and enjoyed the few hours contrast sitting like a bloody millionaire in a cushioned chair, chef's cakes and sandwiches on a table beside him . . . Something good to remember, that would have been. The stuff of fantasy. Still, it was more important to launch his own business. Mindful of the exigencies of the garage roof, Tom put wistful thinking to one side and hurried home.

Half an hour later he was gently easing the Armstrong-Siddeley from the garage. He parked it, with all the precision of a chauffeur used to driving such a car, in the road outside his bungalow. Although its high polish and dazzling chrome were as near perfection as anyone could imagine, Tom was of the opinion that it would be a waste of time merely to stand on guard beside the car waiting for customers. So he fetched his box of dusters the colour of marigolds, and the paler, primrose lengths of chamois leather, and made his way round the familiar body of his beloved machine, re-polishing what had already been re-polished a thousand times. He contemplated switching on the wireless. This, like the dials and the clock, was exquis-itely incorporated into the dashboard – a few inches of knotty golden fabric, above a couple of handsome switches, was the only indication that the complicated mechanics of a wireless were embedded behind the walnut facia. But then he changed his mind: best not to tax the battery, he thought. Best not to ask too much of an old girl on her first outing for a very long time.

So Tom fetched his small black portable radio from indoors, and listened to it while hand and duster made their balletic circles across the dazzling paintwork. On the local news he heard that the response to the QE2's imminent arrival in Ballymorning had been beyond all expectation. People were arriving from all over. On the main road from Dublin, there was a queue outside the town almost a mile long. Visitors were parking on double yellow lines. The local police force was overwhelmed. Supplementary forces were being rushed in to control the traffic. One pub had reportedly already run out of beer. And down at the harbour the crowds were estimated at five hundred. People were warned, said the newscaster, to keep well away from the edge of the harbour wall, lest in the scrum someone should be pushed over the edge.

Wonderful, thought Tom Deary. That was all wonderful, indeed. Just what Ballymorning needed to give the locals a shot in the arm. He stopped his polishing for a moment to look down the street, see if any of the crowds so keen for the QE2 experience might be making their way towards the Armstrong-Siddeley experience – it could be a way of filling in time till the great ship arrived, he thought. If there were so many of them in the shops, as the newscaster had said, then it was unlikely they would miss his advertisement. But the street was empty. Well, to be realistic, it was more likely folk would plan to see the car on their way home. They would want a good place in the queue for the expedition to the QE2: Tom could understand that. Again, a painful wince went through him: what he would have done to be one of the first on a fishing boat, approaching the great white bows of the ship across the water – vast as an iceberg, it must surely be, vast as a skyscraper, and yet a structure that could still be lightly tossed by an angry sea. The kind of thing that made you think, that.

By midday, Tom reckoned there was not a single speck or smear left visible to the human eye. He put away his dusters. He was hungry but, not daring to leave the car unguarded, decided not to go and make himself a sandwich. Instead, he sat in the driving seat, wound down the window. Carefully, he poured lukewarm tea from a flask into a plastic cup, wiping both utensils with a handkerchief to ascertain no wayward drop would slither on to the leather upholstery. The smell of the beige leather provided its usual sense of pleasure: the thickness of the seat behind his back and under his thighs evoked a security that he could not have explained. Through the open window he could just smell the sea, a smell as frail as fine netting. Once, he'd taken a girl called Patricia to a dance in a dress of pale lilac netting, which she called tulle. For some reason, the delicate smell of the sea, nosing into the stuffy air of the car, put him in mind of Patricia – her smile, in particular.

Tom had forgotten to pick up his portable radio from the pavement. Rather than move from his comfortable position, he switched on one of the shining knobs of the car's wireless. From out of the strip of knotty golden fabric came the newscaster's voice, clear as anything.

'The people of Ballymorning, who were expecting the arrival of the QE2 at midday, have just learned from the Lord Mayor that announcements made earlier this morning were by way of an April Fool . . . Hundreds of visitors who had rushed from miles around to witness this spectacle, and indeed to take the trip out to the great ship itself, are said to be bemused, disappointed and even angry. Over now to our reporter in Ballymorning harbour . . .'

Tom, shocked, switched off the radio. He listened to the hollow silence. An April Fool, for heaven's sake. How could he, along with so many others, have been so gullible? How *could* Clive O'Farell have arranged trips around the ship, come to think of it, for all his cheeky daring? What a lot of idiots they all were . . . Even as he smiled to himself, Tom had to deal with a jolt of disappointment within him. He imagined the scenes down at the harbour, the confusion as hundreds of people tried hastily to leave in their inconsiderately parked cars. No wonder some of them found it no laughing matter. Still, the joke had been no bad thing for Ballymorning's locals. Trade in all areas, for a few hours, had been astonishing. And at least some of the disappointed visitors, surely, would make their way up to the Armstrong-Siddeley.

Brisk with hope, Tom got out of the car. In his excitement, he slammed the door more forcefully than he had meant to, and cursed himself. Then he stood to attention, in readiness for his first customer, waiting for the business to begin. Any minute, he thought, possibly dozens of people would arrive, grateful to be afforded some amusement to make up for the disappointment over the QE2, pleased that their journey to Ballymorning had not been wasted after all.

By four that afternoon, still standing stiff as a ceremonial guard by his car, Tom was dizzy, hungry. But when he saw three figures appear at the end of the street, determinedly approaching the Armstrong-Siddeley, all such sensations vanished. There was a man in the middle, a woman on either side of him. As they came nearer, Tom could see the man wore a tartan anorak, and tracksuit of trousers of a particularly offensive maroon. They were made of some kind of slimy material that caught the light. The women – one middle-aged, one in her twenties – were just as offensively dressed in bright, chemical colours. But they were smiling. Tom smiled back, forcing the stiff muscles around his mouth. They stopped, the potential customers, a few yards from where the car and Tom were parked. Tom deemed it wise to let one of them be the first to break the silence.

'Glory be to God, Holy Jasus,' said the man after a while. 'Quite a car you have here. How does your business operate, then?'

'Do we get a five-mile ride? I shall be waving through the window like the Queen,' said one of the women. She disengaged herself from the man, came perilously close to the car's bonnet. She reached out a finger. Very cautiously, as if to judge the quality of a piece of jewellery, she touched its paintwork. Then she quickly withdrew her finger, as if burnt. *There's* polish for you,' she said, to no one in particular. Tom's eyes jumped to the tiny imprint her finger had left, indeterminate as a scrap of cobweb. He longed to take a duster to it, restore perfection. But, sensing that might look like rudeness, he remained where he was.

'You don't get an . . . actual ride in the car,' he said. 'As you can see, she's a very fine antique. I would not want to take the risk over our narrow lanes, now, as I'm sure you can understand.'

The man scratched his head, puzzled. He, too, came dangerously near.

'We read your notice in the Stores,' he said. 'We thought seeing as there's no QE2 we might as well get a ride in a limo.'

'Then I'm sorry you misunderstood the wording,' said Tom. 'It was not meant to suggest there would be a ride. Just a sit down in a remarkable old car, to reflect on the craftsmanship of times past, perhaps . . . For the quality experience,' he said, seeing their faces.

A look of sullen disappointment had now taken the place of the man's smile.

'We've come all the way from bleeding Belfast,' he said. He screwed up a fist and banged the car's bonnet. 'What sort of attraction do you think that is? Sitting in a stationary bloody car?'

Tom wanted to punch the man harder than the man had punched the car. But still he controlled himself, made no attempt to answer the rude question. The tension was broken by a squeal from the young woman. She leapt forward, grabbing the man's arm.

'Don't you see, Dad? You know what this is? It's another April Fool! Two in one day.' She smiled lavishly at Tom.

Her father looked at her. Comprehension began slowly to ooze from his pores. His expression of anger gave way to one of good humour, made sluggish by drink. He laughed, a raw, brutish laugh.

'Good heavens, you're right, too, girl. Place is full of April Fools, I'll say that now. Something to remember. Caught twice . . .' He twinkled at Tom. 'You've pulled off a fine trick, sir. Good luck to you.' He laughed. The women joined him, red mouths pulling back from smoker's teeth. They turned away, linking arms again.

All the way down the street they continued to laugh. As Tom got into the driving seat to return the car for the last time to the garage, he could hear them. He placed his hands evenly on the steering wheel, contemplated the trio through the immaculate windscreen. They shifted from side to side of the pavement, the women supporting the man in his unsteadiness. Their ugly noise still reached him. Tom wound up the window, cutting it off.

Silence returned: safety. Tom started the engine. For a moment he listened to its discreet music, then gently steered the great machine towards the garage. It occurred to him that people so foolish to think that his idea was an April Fool were not the sort of people who would have been any good at describing the trip to the QE2, had that not been an April Fool: and he found this thought was of some comfort.

Mothers
and Fathers

*T*hey had been sitting in the room together for a long time, in silence, unknown to each other, surreptitiously reading signs as strangers do.

He saw a woman in her early forties, an arrogant flare of nostril, fading reddish hair, good cheekbones, floppy beige clothes considerably smarter than those of most of the mothers he encountered on school occasions. She saw a man ten years older than herself, once perhaps handsome, now balding, red silk handkerchief in the pocket of his pinstripe suit indicating a certain flashness that did not match his aristocratic shoes. They continued their silence.

The door opened. The secretary, who earlier had shown them to the room to await their appointments, came in. She was clearly flustered.

'The headmaster's just been on the phone,' she said. 'It seems there's been an accident on the M1. He's stuck in a tailback that goes on for miles. Dreadfully sorry, but hopes you're able to wait. He'll ring again in twenty minutes with a progress report . . .' She kneaded embarrassed hands.

'I'll hang on till then,' said the man.

'So will I,' said the woman.

'Can I press you to a drink?' Both parents shook their

heads. 'Very well. Make yourselves comfortable. I'll be back as soon as I get the next call.'

'Jack Johnson,' said the man, as soon as the secretary had gone.

'April Verner.'

They shook hands, looked at each other more pertinently.

Jack Johnson sighed, took the handkerchief from his pocket and waved it about like a conjurer before dabbing his completely dry forehead.

'Damn nuisance, this. I've come all the way from Lincoln.'

'I've only come from London.' April smiled sympathetically.

'Almost seven-thirty.' He sighed again, petulantly this time. 'You'd have thought he could have made use of his mobile phone a bit earlier, let us know.'

'Perhaps he wasn't quite sure how to use it.'

Jack saw April smile to herself. She had pretty teeth. He looked at her with more interest.

'How do you mean, doesn't know how to use it? Everyone knows how to use a mobile phone. Any man who doesn't know how to use a mobile phone shouldn't be a headmaster.'

Their eyes met.

'Probably you're right,' she said.

'Son here, have you?' asked Jack after a while.

'Two.'

'I've just one left, B Block. Fourth and last, thank heaven, the fees. Little wretch . . . The others were all in the top stream.' The minuscule twitch of his mouth suggested his pride in their achievement, rather than the disappointment in the present little wretch. He flicked at the strap of a gold watch. 'Up to no good, this last one, little monkey. Thought I'd better come and sort things out, see Smiley face to face. Headmasters can be evasive on the telephone, don't you find? So happened I was on my way to the West Country. Would all have been very convenient if it hadn't been for this hold-up.'

'Both of mine are in trouble. One not working – I mean, really not working. The other caught twice in the City by himself. There without permission.' She smiled again.

'Boys will be, and all that,' said Jack, smiling in return.

Their next spell of silence was interrupted by the return of the secretary.

'It's quite hopeless, I'm sorry. Mr Smiley's just rung again to say there's no telling, it may be hours. You mustn't wait. Would you like to make new appointments now, or shall I ring tomorrow?'

'Tomorrow'll do,' said Jack. 'When I'm with my office diary. Most inconvenient.' He shook his head, making sure the secretary was in no doubt of his feelings, indicating just what he thought of a headmaster who goes away on an afternoon when he has appointments with busy parents in the evening, thereby running the risk of failing to keep those appointments. Smiley should have been in school all afternoon, prepared. He should have made absolutely sure he was there.

The secretary, a-dither with more apologies, showed them to the front door. They walked together out into the road, where Jack Johnson's Bentley was parked in front of April Verner's Volvo.

'I've booked myself into The Old Parsonage for the night, matter of fact. Lovely place, always stop there when I have a chance,' said Jack. 'Why don't you come and have a drink before you go back to London? We could even have a bite to eat.'

April hesitated. She was hungry, tired. It had been a long and busy day at the office. No time for lunch. No time for shopping. Empty fridge at home. Empty house. Martin off somewhere in France, setting up one of his deals that necessitated Marilyn, his personal assistant, being there too.

'Lovely,' she said. 'I'd like that.'

In return for a drink and a sandwich, she was prepared to put up with almost any kind of company, even this tetchy father for whose fourth son she felt instinctive pity.

In the bar of The Old Parsonage, they sat at the small, polished table, previously booked for one, in a corner. April looked round at the hazy colours of the room, with its lively wood fire and myriad pictures on the walls, and a curious sense of luxury possessed her. These days, she was rarely asked out for a drink. Spontaneous adventures, the essence of her youth, had long since ceased. No matter how dreadful Jack Johnson, and she didn't like the way he waved ostentatiously at the waiter with a fat hand, she was determined to enjoy the next hour.

'Bottle of champagne – how about that? We need some-thing to calm us down. Wretched fellow, Smiley, messing us about like this.'

April nodded. She longed for champagne.

'How about bagels and smoked salmon? They do it jolly

well here. Or the lobster ravioli, would you rather? Mind you leave room for the tiramisu.'

It was fun, choosing what to eat, though when she gave herself a moment to analyse the fun April realised it was the nefarious element more than the company that appealed to her. Here she was in Oxford, having supper with a fellow parent because the headmaster had not turned up . . . and Martin had no idea. Not all that wicked, really.

'Let's get through the CV,' Jack was saying, as they sipped the dry champagne. 'I'm a printer. Businesses all over the place. Lot of travelling about. Live in Lincolnshire, one wife, four sons. You?'

April hoped that after two rather large gulps of her drink she could be equally succinct.

'I'm a barrister. Specialise in divorce.' She saw Jack's eyebrows briefly clench. 'Just the two sons, as I said, both still here. My husband's in the import–export business – can't say I know a great deal about it. It means he has to go abroad a lot. He's in Paris at the moment.' With Marilyn, she didn't say.

'That's us, then,' said Jack, filling glasses. 'Jolly good. Now we can get on to something interesting.'

No immediate subject sprang to either of their minds, but halfway through their ravioli they found themselves ruminating on the one topic they had in common – parenthood.

'I suppose we're all bloody awful mothers and fathers, no matter how good our intentions to be otherwise,' ventured Jack. The champagne-induced pinkness of April Verner's cheeks appealed to him. 'Nature of parenthood. Nothing but failure and disappointment. Well, I go too far. When they do well, it's jolly satisfying. And I have to say my eldest three are a bright lot, conscientious. Suppose they got their brains from their mother – she's a scientist. I was never a scholar myself, nothing very brainy about Jack Johnson. Except when it comes to business. I'm a businessman through and through. Love it, the cut and thrust, the money. But young Simon, the little wretch I'd come down to talk about – he's a funny lad. Bit of a flibberty-gibbet, like me. Bit of a depressive . . . Don't know what's got into him these last couple of years. He's a worry, to tell the truth.' Jack paused to fill their glasses. 'Could be, I suppose, not quite ideal conditions at home these days, getting to him. Sheila and I seem to . . . have our disagreements. Think Simon's got it in mind we may be going to get divorced. Well, that's not so, but I'm damned if I know how to convince him. Awkward sort of subject. I'm not much good at that sort of thing.'

'My two are always asking why their father is away so much,' said April, after a while. 'I mean, they know it's business, his work. But it's as if they have their suspicions.'

'And might they be right?'

'No.' Lying to a stranger was better than disloyalty to a husband, for all his unfaithfulness.

'That's good. Ravioli all right?'

'Delicious.'

'You can't hide much from children. They're canny little buggers, see much more than you suppose.'

'True.'

'You're a damn pretty woman, if I may say so.'

'Thank you.'

'Are you on for the tiramisu?'

'Please. I'm something of a chocolate freak.'

'Cream's my undoing. You'll never convert me to this crème fraîche business. Sheila's always saying I'll end up with a heart attack. But a man can't be expected to give up all treats, can he?'

April's silence showed she felt the question to be rhetorical. In fact, her head was so fizzing with small explosions of light that it would have been beyond her to give the silly question a considered answer. Through the scintillating veil before her eyes, she saw her host as he must have been some twenty years ago, before his love of cream had pouched the skin around his jaw and the business lunches had reddened his cheeks. Her thoughts then turned to Martin. He was not a generous man. He would not consider it economically sound to spend money on champagne for his girlfriend. Somewhere in France, Marilyn would be sipping *vin ordinaire*. April felt unusually happy.

With the tiramisu, they had a second bottle of champagne. The chocolate seemed to have a sobering effect on the alcohol.

'What I always wonder,' said April, 'is how much example rubs off on our children? I mean, if they see their parents working hard, does this mean they follow suit, or determine to behave quite differently? Our two are far from stupid – in fact, both are particularly good at maths. But they say that judging by us hard work isn't all that rewarding – what can they mean by that, I wonder? They say it means we're away so much. Or if we're there we're always so preoccupied, not concentrating enough on them. Talk is nothing but plans, they say. There are few peaceful times.' She paused. 'The sad thing is, they're right.'

Jack briefly patted April's hand.

'You'd better have a lot of coffee before driving home.'

'I will.'

'Or, you could stay.' He watched her face, unable to read signals.

April found the idea uninteresting, but she was very tired. She did not like the thought of the drive home. Perhaps Jack meant she should take a room herself . . . though by the look on his face, he didn't.

'I've a charming room. The one, it's said, where Oscar Wilde discovered his proclivities.'

April smiled. If the example of parents rubbed off on to their children, then his four sons must be a pompous lot, she thought. Jack, taking her expression to mean acceptance, pressed her hand rather than patted it this time.

'I don't want to appear presumptuous,' he said. 'That's the last thing I want. Two strangers brought together by the non-appearance of a headmaster . . . very rum, but could just be our good luck. Shall I see if they have a room for you?'

That was rather nice of him, thought April, her head still afloat, her body deliquescent from the warmth of the fire. Considerate. A kind man. Martin far away with Marilyn. Too weary to listen to arguments within her, suddenly the fight went out of her.

'Don't bother,' she said.

April was intrigued by the bedroom, transformed from

the spartan place of Wilde's day. Everything had been thought of: safe, clock, magnificent Italian shower in the marble bathroom, fridge full of drinks, comfortable arm-chair, interlined curtains, fruit and flowers.

'Amazing,' she said. Exploring the place slowly enabled her to postpone the future imperfect, the awkwardness of making the next move towards the night in the large bed.

'I can see you're not used to hotels, this sort of thing.'

'No.'

'Ah.' Evidently Jack was.

As the champagne began to ebb, giving way to the clar-ity of mind induced by black coffee, April began to see the scene in all its horror. She had become a mere pawn in what was a normal way of life to Jack Johnson: trips away from home meant automatically picking up any available woman. He sat heavily on the bed.

'I won't lay a finger on you,' he said, 'if that's what you want.'

The horror receded: he was a man of surprises. April now felt she had maligned him. He wasn't simply a ruthless seducer, after all. In fact, he seemed a lonely man. Rather sad. And it had been a very generous dinner. A question, so often struggled with in her youth, came back to April – was he owed payment for such a dinner? What should she do? Even now, there was time to go.

April shut herself in the bathroom to confront herself. Twenty minutes later, she reappeared in the white towelling bathrobe provided by the hotel. Jack was watching the television, drinking whisky. He looked up, appraising.

'Parents,' he said, and laughed a little grimly.

The next morning, Jack Johnson and April Verner took breakfast at the same table, with its comfortable chairs, where they had dined the night before. A new fire was burning, pale bars of sun sloped across the white-clothed tables.

Jack had to be in Bristol at ten. He kept glancing at his watch. April was free until the afternoon, when she had a meeting in Chambers. She felt inclined, on so temperate a day, to linger in Oxford a while, walk through Magdalen deer parks, perhaps. See if the fritillaries were out.

'Well,' said Jack. The inner battle between impatience to be off and the desire to remain polite to the end of this assignation caused sweat to froth on his temples. He signalled for the waiter, the bill, no less ostentatiously than he had the night before. Between them they had eaten a whole basket of warm bread rolls and croissants baked at dawn.

'I must be off.'

'I might stay a while.'

'You do that. Another cappuccino? Read the papers.' He stood up. 'Very nice to have met you.' He leant down, kissed April on the cheek. She felt his dampness, was repelled by the sweetness of his aftershave. 'Could be we'll meet again at our next appointments with Smiley . . .' He put a small white card beside April's plate: business address and numbers. 'Call me if you feel like it, won't you?'

Then Jack Johnson picked up his smart little overnight case with its expensive leather straps and was gone.

April tore the card into minute pieces which she mixed with the crumbs on her plate. Tonight Martin would be home and she would insist, this time, that he came with her to see the headmaster. Tonight he would tell her in jovial detail about his trip to France, only omitting to mention the presence of Marilyn. He would probably forget to ask what the headmaster had said about the boys. It certainly wouldn't occur to him to ask how she had spent her evening. In the same way that trust makes infidelity easy to accomplish, so does lack of interest in a spouse's activities. In Addison Walk, an hour later, April remembered the hopes she had entertained on many such walks as an undergraduate. Love, interest, a liveliness of being as man and wife, the mutual, buoyant pleasure of being parents.

On the journey back to London, April relived the gropings of the night and laughed herself to scorn. It was only the second time she had been unfaithful in fifteen years: she should have treated herself, at least, to a better lover. Physically churlish, Jack Johnson had been, and she had had no heart to encourage him in less selfish ways. But, far worse than his ungracious thudding, had been later to see him sleep so quickly beside her, apparently unmoved by a stranger in the bed. He had snored, tossed crudely about in sleep, snatching the sheets from her side. At dawn, April, who had not slept at all, crept out for a bath and dressed. She could not face lying beside his early-morning face, ruddy manifestation of her mistake.

Within days of returning to home and working life, the horrible night disappeared. She could not remember Jack's features, his hands, his voice. And even when she returned to the school some months later, for Sports Day, the sight of him failed at first to re-ignite her guilt.

She saw him in the distance, a cross-looking woman in

skinny spectacles by his side. He still wore the red hand-kerchief: this time it flopped from the pocket of a creased linen suit. Martin, by April's side, followed her gaze.

'Never ceases to fascinate me,' he said. 'You look at the children, then at their parents, and you understand instantly why those children are like they are.' Three plump boys had joined Jack Johnson. They hung about with the important look of old boys returning to their prep school. A small, skinny one clung to the woman. The little wretch, April supposed, her pity renewed. Then they were lost from sight in the crowd.

She next saw Jack lined up for the fathers' race: jacket off, silk shirt darkened with melon slices of sweat under the arms.

'Not much competition there,' said Martin and went to stand beside Jack.

April and her two boys found themselves next to the Johnson wife and children among the spectators. April observed the resigned mouth of Mrs Johnson – the hunched shoulders and bloodless hands, while Martin ran an easy race to beat the rest of the motley field. Jack, she saw, lumbered up second from last.

April, as much as her sons, enjoyed Martin's win (third year running) and found herself laughing, joining the con-gratulations as he put an arm around her shoulders. From the corner of her eye, she saw Jack Johnson dab his face with the red handkerchief and wave. April gave the small-est nod of recognition, dismissing him so entirely in her mind that there was no time to wonder, for the hundredth time, how she could ever have been so unwise.

Martin's arm continued to rest around her shoulders. Since Marilyn had moved to some other company, his infatuation had waned and he was exercising his charms on April, which was often his way between infidelities. At such times, she found forgiveness easy. The love she usually felt it necessary to withhold from her husband she bestowed willingly on him again, hoping it could remain thus for a month or so.

'Tell you what,' Martin was saying to her and the boys, 'I've booked a table for dinner before we drive back, some hotel I heard was the Algonquin of Oxford. All right?' His eyes met April's. She could think of no reason to refuse, and nodded.

The bar of The Old Parsonage was filled with parents and their children that night, celebrating the end of another term, another year. For some, the junction between the end of preparatory school before the step to public school. Around the small polished tables, family life abounded noisily, happily. Martin chose April's favourite white wine without asking. From time to time, her eyes travelled among the very disparate mothers and fathers. The relief she felt that Jack Johnson and his wife were not among them registered lightly as a shadow on her warm skin and, in the kind light of the evening, she liked to think it was only the innocence of her sons that made her want to cry.

Laughter in

the Willows

*I*t was Isabel Loughland's second summer up at Oxford and in her own mind she was a failure. This feeling had come to her within weeks of arriving at New College, and settled more deeply every term. It was nothing to do with her studies. That part of her life, mercifully, was rewarding. She worked hard, taking advantage of hours unoccupied by romantic interest, and the results were encouraging. If she carried on like this, she had been advised, there was a chance she would get a good second-class degree – even a first.

This thought was no compensation for a loveless life. The few girlfriends Isabel had made had paired off with men very soon after they arrived. By now, initial partners had changed and changed again. Keeping up with the shuffle of love affairs was at first entertaining (how Isabel admired their ability to be so positive of their attraction to one, and then so quickly to another). Now it was wearying. She no longer bothered. She had become used to being a lone figure in a coupled society, and reckoned a change in this situation was unlikely. Among the dozens of male undergraduates she had encountered, not a single one had caused her the ungrounding that she knew to be the prime indication of love.

Isabel felt no self-pity: merely, puzzlement. The men who had made advances to her – and even now, when the fear of committing sexual harassment makes for some hesitation, there was no shortage of them – had claimed her as pretty, almost beautiful. Certainly she was a good listener – her mother had taught her there was no aphrodisiac so potent as lending an attentive ear. She could make people laugh. She was the provider of imaginative gestures; she was modest and sympathetic.

The stumbling block, she knew, was the *unfashionable* air that blew off her, awesome as expensive scent. She did not dress like the others, in jeans and grubby layered things, and elephantine boots. She wore long, clean skirts of pure cotton or velvet, and pumps of pale kid. She brushed her hair and, in summer, wore straw hats stuck with real flowers to evensong. Her demeanour gave clues to her limitations. She had no desire to become close to a man after a single drink in The Blue Boar (although she was not averse to a pint of lager), and any suggestions of a kiss on immediate acquaintance were politely turned down. It was not that she was a prude – when the time came, she was convinced she would make love as keenly as her friends. But she was of the outdated belief that the only chance of a lasting relationship was friendship that developed into love and sex: the other way round did not augur well for permanency. While mere lust did not interest her, the height of her ideals caused her disillusion. Several times, her hopes were raised in the direction of a particular figure, only to be crushed by his expectations of instant physical gratification.

She should have been born in a different age, Isabel

reflected, as she did so often. On this fine evening, sitting by herself in New College gardens, she imagined the attraction of life at Jane Austen's pace: the *containing* of realisation. That's what she sought. That was the essence of the romance she believed in.

Isabel picked daisies from the perimeter of her rug. She tried to remember how to make a chain. Various couples walked by, caught up in the kind of rapture which, in her judgement, was too self-conscious to be anything more than temporary. She felt no envy: that was not what she wanted. But disappointment on finding no one of the stuff she imagined, in almost two years at Oxford, was sometimes acute. Now, for instance. It was a waste of such an evening, not to be sharing it. Returning to books was sometimes not enough.

The lilacs, nearby, were beginning to unfurl. Blossom snowed down from a cherry tree. Shadows had stretched almost to the edge of the rug. (Isabel was ridiculed for her rug, with its mackintosh backing.) Others, nearby, sat on the grass. Time to go in, she thought. Back to her room. An evening of more study.

She looked up. A single man – a rare sight on a fine summer's evening in college grounds – was coming towards her. He was exceptionally thin, narrow. From a distance, his face was a blade. He wore pale baggy trousers of crushed linen, as if he'd just discovered *Brideshead*. Isabel smiled at the thought. She recognised him. Last week in chapel she had dropped her prayer book. He had picked it up, returned it to her. In the brief moment of the handing over, their eyes had met without interest.

It was evident, in the firmness of his step, that he was not about to pass by. He was intent on speaking.

Isabel shifted slightly, indicating reluctance to be encountered. She wanted to continue with her quiet evening, not have to make the effort to turn down an invitation.

The man was by her now. A concave figure, holding out his hand – an unusual gesture among students. Isabel shook it, surprised by such unaccustomed formality, but good manners instinctive within her.

'Jacques,' he said, 'de Noailles. We met in chapel last Sunday evening. I've been looking for you.'

Isabel suppressed a small sigh. She could not be unbent by flattery.

'Isabel Loughland,' she said reluctantly. 'This is my college.'

Jacques lowered himself, unasked, on to the grass beside the rug. It did not occur to Isabel to invite him to share it.

'I'm at Corpus.' Jacques de Noailles leant back on his elbows, shut his eyes. In the instant that they were shut, Isabel observed a veil of pure evil cross his face. Or perhaps it was a strand of shade extending, now that it was almost eight, from the lilacs. There was something intriguing in the way his narrow chest dipped deeply towards his spine. She liked the cornflower blue of his clean shirt.

He opened his eyes, made no attempt to smile at her.

'Greats,' he said. 'How about you?'

'Mediaeval History.'

'That was an option for me. I would have liked that. But my father said, don't miss your chance of philosophies. He's French. You know what eager philosophers the French are.'

Isabel put down the book she had picked up in readiness to leave before Jacques had arrived.

'Yes,' she said.

'Strange: this is my third year and last Sunday was the first time I've seen you,' said Jacques.

'Not so very strange, so many . . . It's only my second year.'

'Ah.' They talked about their undergraduate lives for a while, and their vacations. Jacques said he divided his time between his mother in Scotland and his father in Provence. After coming down from Oxford, he said, he intended to take a course at the Sorbonne. Isabel told him she lived in Devon. Both her parents were botanists, often away in foreign mountains in search of extraordinary species. She and Jacques did not ask each other many questions. They took it in turns to offer small pieces of information, giving little away.

An hour passed. It had grown cool. Jacques raised himself on to his haunches, made ready to go.

'I was just wondering – is there anything in Oxford that you haven't done in your two years here? That you would like to do? It's difficult to come up with an original invitation. But I'm sorry. Silly question. It was only that I thought a girl like you must have done *everything*.'

Isabel felt herself blush. She let a long moment pass. Dare she tell him? Yes, she decided.

'As a matter of fact, there is one thing. It's so . . . childish. Such a cliché. It's what everyone does in their first summer, but somehow the chance never came. I want to go on a punt . . .'

Jacques did not laugh, as she had expected.

'Well, for that matter, I've never been on one either,' he said. 'It's never occurred to me. *Alors!* We shall go on a punt. I shall make arrangements.'

He stood, very quickly, rubbing his long thin thighs with his long thin hands. He pulled Isabel to her feet.

'Politically incorrect, I dare say.' They both laughed. 'You're taller than I expected.' He swooped down again, as if embarrassed by the intimacy of the spontaneous observation, and picked up the daisy chain. For a moment, Isabel thought he intended to take it: an unlikely romantic gesture. But he gave it back to her, dangling it lightly across her wrist. 'Now, I must go.'

Dusk had covered the grass, thickened the trees.

The next morning, Isabel found a message at the Lodge. *Be at Magdalen Bridge at three p.m. Bring your rug. Jacques.*

Impertinent, the rug bit, she thought. Though not impertinent enough to refuse the invitation.

She lay back in the punt, eyes half closed. All was just as she had imagined. Her rug was spread over cushions supplied by Jacques who tussled, tight-lipped, with the pole. Isabel pretended not to notice his lack of talent as a punter, and did not mind how long it took, the journey down the river. The heat of the sun and plash of water made her sleepy, too sleepy to speak.

At some moment, it might have been an hour after they set off, Jacques announced they had arrived. Isabel, rousing herself, saw they had tied up at the bank beside an enormous willow tree.

'I'd say that was pretty good for someone who's never done it before,' she said, sitting up.

'Thanks. But you were asleep most of the time.'

'Half asleep.'

They lifted out the rug, cushions and a small wicker hamper. This made Isabel laugh.

'Most undergraduate picnics travel in plastic bags,' she said.

'I don't like plastic bags.' Jacques' shirt was dark with sweat. 'If you're going to take a picnic at all, you might as well bother, no? What do you think of this place? Do you like it?'

Isabel looked across the river. The meadows were that bright green of early May with a pointillist covering of cow parsley. Distant woods of new, transparent leaves made delicate fans against the sky.

'Good,' she said.

'And the willow? You like this old tree? It's famous. Lots of people come here. We're lucky to have it to ourselves.'

'You've been here before, then?'

'Oh yes, often. But never by punt. I've always walked.' He answered lightly. A sudden positioning of shadow on his face reminded Isabel of last night's brief illusion of cruelty. He was smiling. Remembering? Who had he come with? With what intent? Questions leapt in Isabel's mind, but they were empty. She wondered slightly at her lack of curiosity.

Jacques parted the thickly-leaved branches of the willow. Isabel followed him into the ribboned vault beneath it. Grass was scant here, worn away by previous visitors.

There were other signs of the popularity of the hiding place, too. An empty crisp bag, a scrunched-up beer can.

'Bastards,' said Jacques. He picked up the rubbish, went back through the branches to bury it. Alone for a moment in this place of gently shifting leaf shadow, Isabel clutched herself with crossed arms. She felt a distant chill. The heat of the sun could not penetrate the walls of the greenery, though it made a million fireflies among the leaves, points of lights that dazzled as they moved with the slight breeze. Isabel wondered if she should suggest they should eat outside.

Jacques returned.

'So hot. This is wonderful, no? The cool.'

They laid out the rug and cushions. The hamper was unpacked. Jacques had *bothered*: there was proper French bread, and *millefeuilles* from the Maison Blanc; pâtés, tiny cheeses in oiled paper tied with twine. Black misted grapes, a bottle of white wine, red gingham napkins and china plates.

'Is all right? Enough?'

'It's fine. It's wonderful. You've gone to such trouble.'

They ate slowly, almost in silence. Isabel revelled in the delicious food, and the way Jacques handed her a piece of baguette with small yellow tomatoes balancing on a wedge of *pâté de campagne*. But she still wished they were outside on the riverbank, despite the heat. The chill beneath the tree continued to strike: the bleak chill of milk bottles on a cold winter doorstep, the dank chill of turgid water – she could not quite place the exact kind of coldness, but it made goose pimples on her bare arms. Isabel pulled on her cardigan. Two glasses of wine had made her sleepy again. She longed to lie back on the cushions, but feared this would look like an untoward invitation. Then, eyes on Jacques' serious profile – he was eating a *millefeuille* with his fingers, forks being the only thing he had forgotten – she realised that no such thought would occur to him. She felt confident of that, though could not explain to herself why . . .

So she lay back, let her eyes trail among the long streamers of leaf that dangled from the branches above her. Focussing more sharply, she could see each one as an individual, with its just visible webbing of veins, its fragile whiplash of spine. There was grey in the various greens, through which the fireflies of sunlight splattered lemony freckles. A sudden gust of breeze made chaotic shadows dance on Jacques' blue shirt.

'Strobe shadows,' said Isabel, more to herself than to him.

Jacques turned to her, one side of curious mouth, awash with *crème patissière*, lifted in agreement.

'Strobe shadows,' he said.

Isabel was grateful for his instant understanding. She fell asleep.

She was woken by laughter. It took her a moment to re-orient herself. Willow tree: picnic: Jacques: that was it. Where was he? The picnic things had been cleared away, the wicker hamper closed and buckled. The neatness pleased her, but she was still cold. The shade under the tree was more intense.

Isabel sat up, looked at her watch. Five o'clock. She must

have slept for at least an hour. A waste, really. But also agreeable. To be able to fall asleep in the presence of a little-known acquaintance who has taken such trouble with a picnic, she was thinking, when she heard the laughter again. A man's, a young woman's. Clashing, chiming. People outside. People seeking shade, perhaps. They would come in, blasting her solitude. There would be awkwardness, embarrassment. Please don't let us disturb you . . . No, no, not at all . . . do come in. Well, how lucky she and Jacques had been for a few hours, Isabel thought. To have had such a popular place to themselves was obviously a piece of good fortune.

She stood up, brushed an insect from her skirt. Head bowed, concentrating, she did not see Jacques return through the branches. When she looked up and saw him before her, she felt surprise. His face, reddened by the sun, was shredded by the straggling shadows of the willow leaves.

'I went for a walk along the tow-path,' he said.

'I'm sorry I slept so long.'

'I'm glad you did. But time to go now. The slow journey back.' He gave a smile that flickered with moving shadow. 'Perhaps I'll do better.'

'Others have arrived, anyway,' said Isabel.

'Didn't see anyone.'

'I heard laughter. Not a moment ago.'

'There was no one out there.'

'Maybe they were just walking by.'

'Well, never mind. We must go.'

Jacques bent to pick up the hamper. A distinct peal of

laughter came from behind Isabel. She jumped round. No one. Nothing.

'There,' she said.

'People playing silly games,' said Jacques. 'Can you manage the rug and the cushions? We'll leave it to them. They can come in now.'

'But the laughter was in here.'

'You're imagining things. People queue up for this place. It's no longer a secret, unfortunately. They come in here to – well, have their fun.'

He led the way through the branches. As Isabel followed him, the long leaves tickled her face with a disagreeable touch. Out on the bank again, she felt relief. A still-hot sun gushed over her: gratifying, comforting warmth that made her shiver pleasantly. The brown water of the river spread taut beneath the waiting punt. A lark sang high above them.

On the way back, Jacques said, 'There's a punting party in a few weeks' time. A whole crowd of us. Would you like to come? It's fancy dress, I'm afraid. Dressing up in Edwardian gear – some silly idea. An awful bother, I think.'

'Nostalgia's so fashionable,' said Isabel. 'Yes, I'd love to.'

'You'll have to find something – some old dress, some fancy hat, put your hair up.'

'I'll rather enjoy that.'

'We'll go together, then.'

By the time they tied up at Magdalen Bridge, the sky was a deep denim blue behind the tower. Crowds of punters were laughing, drinking, eating ice-creams.

*

Isabel found a second-hand shop near the station. She was trying to make her choice. It was dreadfully hot, stuffy. There was a smell of mothballs, old garments, dead starch. The walls were hung with dresses whose heyday was several decades ago, their gold embroidery and lace panels a little battered, but their spirits not extinguished. There was nothing suitable for the punting picnic, the kind of Edwardian tea-gown Isabel had in mind.

'Just got a new bundle in,' said the woman in charge, dumping a pile of twisted clothes on the counter. 'You can see if there's anything you like if you want to look through these.'

Isabel began to rummage through them. They were pale, faded colours, summery stuffs, torn and frayed, some of them, and very crumpled. Within moments, her eyes lighted on a piece of creamy muslin dotted with faint forget-me-nots: she pulled it from the pile. It was exactly what she was after, demure and pretty with small lace Vs that protruded from the long sleeves to cover the back of the hand. All it needed was a sash of palest blue moiré . . . Isabel felt reckless with excitement: the dress was more than she had intended to spend, but she did not care. A picture was beginning to form in her mind – a little hazy, but something to do with seduction, at last, in this dress. Something to do with *possibility*, and Jacques.

Back in her room, she shook out the dress and studied it more carefully: the hand-sewn hems of tiny stitches, the coarse hooks and eyes of the day, the enchanting fabric itself. She hung it over her chair, skirt spread out so that it touched the floor. Then she hurried off to Browns where, for the third time since their expedition on the punt, she was to have tea with Jacques. To date, there had been no invitations for anything later in the day. Things were progressing at just the pace so appreciated by Isabel. With each formal date – snippets of information accumulating – anticipation fizzed a little more: there was reason, Isabel began to think, for hope.

When she returned to her room at about six-thirty in the evening, her immediate impression was of the lack of air. It had been a very hot day, but she had left the window shut, being on the ground floor, for security: it was not unknown for undergraduates to rob each other these days.

On her way to the window Isabel's eyes fell on the dress – of which she had made no mention to Jacques. It was to be a surprise. It was not as she had left it. Slumped considerably to one side, so small a part of the bodice was now propped up against the back of the chair that the slightest movement would have caused it to fall completely.

This was strange. How could this have happened? There was no breath of air in the room. The door had been locked: no one had been in. Isabel's mind raced uneasily before quickly she found an explanation. Someone must have been running in the passage outside . . . the vibration of feet on old boards. All the same, her heart quickened. In the stifling room, the dress looked so desolate she felt a moment's chill. Goose pimples stood up on her bare arms, just as they had when she heard the laughter in the willows.

Scoffing at herself, Isabel picked up the dress with some distaste. She put it on a hanger. The muslin skirt, so soft and dry in the shop, felt slimy against her hands. Almost damp.

Isabel hung it on the outside of the wardrobe. To check that she had been imagining the inexplicable dampness, she forced herself to screw up the frill on the hem with both hands. Obviously, her imagination had been playing tricks. The material was warm, dry, smelling faintly of musty flowers. Cowslips, Isabel thought. She opened the window, took out her books. She sat down at her desk, her back to the dress, wanting to put it from her mind.

But in the next few weeks before the punting party, it caused her some disturbance. She washed it, ironed it, skilfully mended a couple of small tears. All these jobs she found disagreeable: the silly thought came to her that by restoring it to its pristine condition she was somehow intruding. She bought a long blue moiré ribbon which she tied round the waist, a beautiful sash. Then, fearful of crushing it in the crowded wardrobe, she left the dress hanging outside. Each time she returned to her room she was greeted by its hanging presence – a presence more potent than an ordinary piece of clothing on a hanger. Always, she could swear, its position was fractionally changed – she made sure to straighten it before she left, and when she came back it had invariably shifted a little to one side or the other. This change was almost imperceptible, but Isabel's conviction that it *was* a change grew stronger every day. In her alarmed state, she began to imagine that in her absence the garment put up some kind of a struggle. Others, coming to her room, admired it, of course. Handsome symbol of another age, they said: imagine wearing something that prissy today.

Gradually, Isabel herself began to dread coming back to

her room. The greeting from the still dress that moved when she was out became harder to ignore by concentrating on her work. She could not bring herself to try it on: she knew instinctively it would fit. And once the punting party was over, she began to think, she would re-sell the dress, throwing in the expensive sash as an added bonus.

Every few days, Jacques and Isabel met for the same teas – scones and cream and strawberry jam – in Browns, and Jacques unbent a little. One afternoon, he went so far as to suggest Isabel might like to visit his father's house in the Luberon in the vacation. Perhaps, Isabel replied. What she meant was, perhaps the time was coming for things to speed up a little.

'You would like,' he said.

'I expect I would.'

Their conversations were not marked by vitality. Rather, they shifted at a gentle pace, as does the talk of two people, bound by affection, who have known each other well for many years. Isabel found this comforting.

On the day before the punting party, they did not meet. Isabel spent many hours, in her disciplined way, getting ahead with work: she did not want the thought of an essay on Anna Comnena hanging over her as the gathering of punts drifted down the Cherwell . . . Tired by the evening, the essay accomplished, books neatly stacked, she went to bed soon after nine and slept at once.

She woke at three a.m. A thin spear of moonlight through the window had lighted on the waiting dress (re-ironed two days ago), bleaching its creamy colour to a milky whiteness, giving it a cloudy volume as if invisible thighs shifted beneath it. She distinctly saw it move.

Cold, Isabel sat up. Now, as her eyes grew accustomed to the fragile darkness, she could see the bodice and the long limp sleeves that seemed not as limp as the sleeves of an empty dress should be. It was the dress that had woken her, she was quite sure of that, with its sudden, living presence.

Terrified, Isabel switched on the light. At once she saw how foolish she had been: the dress was ordinary again, beautifully ironed, waiting, unmoving. The illusion of moments before must have been the tail-end of a nightmare. She smiled at herself, heart thumping: by now, she thought, she knew Jacques well enough to tell him of the strange experience, and of the odd feelings she had about the dress. Maybe there would be a chance tomorrow. Calmer, but not liking to put out the light, she picked up a book and read till dawn.

The following evening, when the time came to change, Isabel opened her door on to the corridor. In some amorphous way, she wanted the reassurance of others nearby: the scurrying down the corridor, the heads looking in to check on progress. Now Isabel was seen by her friends to be 'in a relationship' too, they treated her with less polite kindness. This evening, finally in the dress, sash bow perfectly tied, muslin underskirt soft against her legs, she was grateful for their crude comments concerning virgin spinsters, and their coarse admiration of her finished appearance. She had piled up her hair in an Edwardian bun: on top of this she put her mother's wedding hat, a period concoction of silk roses clambering over creamy straw, with a tiny veil that half hid her eyes. A velvet ribbon she wore around her throat, to which she had pinned a small star. She was ready.

'You look much more the part than any of us,' said one of her friends. 'But then you've never been of this age.'

Isabel, arranging the Vs of lace over the backs of her hands, blushed. She felt intensely happy. All the misgivings about the dress, the absurd feelings of unease it had caused her, had vanished. She knew it suited her, that she looked well in it. And this was the sort of occasion she had been waiting for so hopelessly for five terms. *This* was the Oxford of her most extravagant imaginings.

It was seven p.m. when she joined a group of girls in long floating dresses to walk to Magdalen Bridge where Jacques, and other dates, would be waiting. Isabel's normal modesty was taxed: she could not help feeling she was the *belle dame* of the group. The others had strived, but somehow failed, in their attempts at Edwardian gear. They wore long shabby dresses with Doc Marten boots beneath. Some of them had piled up their hair, though nothing would disguise the contemporary haughtiness of their expressions, and their language would have been almost incomprehensible to those of the Edwardian era. But they were in high spirits, looking forward to a night of drink and music and love beneath the stars, when their fancy dresses would be ruined on the damp banks of the Cherwell.

At the meeting place there was a huge gathering of yet more girls in long dresses and men, transformed in appearance by striped blazers, cream trousers and boaters stuck with flowers. They bore no resemblance to the seedy, be-jeaned lot of normal day. There was much shrieking and incredulous laughter as food and bottles and ghetto blasters were handed into the punts.

'I thought of bringing my gramophone,' said Jacques, suddenly at Isabel's side, 'but I didn't think it would be appreciated.' His eyes moved politely up and down her dress. He made no comment, but gave her shoulder the briefest squeeze. All around them, others were already greeting each other with greedy kisses on the lips. Jacques had wisely not volunteered to be a punter. This meant he and Isabel could sit side by side, idle passengers, their attention free for the delights of the journey downriver.

By the time the convoy of punts set off, the sky was a deep blue-green, tipped with such refulgent clouds that Isabel imagined a giant peacock, standing on the horizon, had simply raised its fan-shaped tail to the heavens . . . As Magdalen Tower disappeared, and a tunnel of greenery loomed, she found herself sipping pink champagne, Jacques' arm about her. She could feel the boniness of his side. They had never been so close before. Nor had Isabel ever felt such irresponsible deliquescence: no matter what he asked her, tonight, she would agree. They had waited long enough.

Even as the party took place, Isabel was aware of that quality of luminescence that usually touches the memory of things past rather than present reality. She clutched each moment to herself, wanting to preserve it in all its detail. She was not, after all, a girl so used to parties that circumstances had to be particularly vivid to cause the kind of impression that cannot fade. The wonder was increased by the constant presence of Jacques by her side. They shared her rug for the picnic on the bank by the willow, now a familiar place. A half-moon rose in the jade-black sky, its face smeared by unhurried clouds. Someone had brought jars containing candles, which were lighted in random spots, and a man with no apparent girlfriend (Isabel's heart went out to him in 'sublime compassion') sat playing a melancholy tune on his flute.

'This is very mad, very English,' Jacques said. He was folding dismal threads of ham into a piece of bread for Isabel. The food was not of the same standard as the previous picnic, but there was no shortage of pink champagne.

Once seated and eating, the chattering of the undergraduates lost its shrillness. It was as if, awed by the density of the warm night, intoxicated by the smells of ripe hay and damp long grass, they tempered their voices. Such innocence! Jacques replied, when Isabel whispered these thoughts to him. It was just that a good deal of drink and dope has already been consumed, he said. But it seemed to Isabel that the voices were quieter. It was always possible to hear the flute among them.

When the picnic was finished, more cigarettes and joints were lighted. One punt, bearing two couples, set off uncertainly into the darkness. Those left on the bank switched on a tape of rock music and began barefoot to dance. This enraged the others, who thought such crudeness broke the spell of the age they were trying to recreate, and sentimental tunes from the 30s were put on instead.

'Still wrong,' pointed out Jacques, 'but I suppose we can't dance to *The Last Rose of Summer*.'

He helped Isabel to her feet, but not to dance.

'I'm not much good,' he said. 'No sense of rhythm. Let's see what's happening under our tree.'

They stepped from the moody darkness of the riverbank into the thicker gloom beneath its branches. On the ground were more jars of candles, the light not strong enough to turn the long leaves into ribbon shadows, as the fierce sun had managed on their last visit. Several couples were lying together, oblivious of each other, of everyone. Girls squirmed, long skirts thrown back over their knees. They lay on striped blazers, covered by thrusting flannel haunches: mouths locked.

'I told you,' said Jacques.

Isabel was glad of the darkness. She felt herself stiffen, blush. She was suddenly awkward. Jacques took her hand, led her back outside.

'What would you like to do? Dance with someone else?'

'Just watch,' said Isabel.

They took a bottle, the rug and cushions, and made themselves comfortable in one of the moored punts. They watched the dancing and embracing under gently changing patterns of moon and cloud. The music, thin recordings of sad love songs, fluttered down to them. They did not speak.

Isabel, on purpose, had not brought her watch. So she had no idea what precise moment of the night Jacques stirred, and concentrated on rubbing his ankle, which he had bruised some days before.

'I suppose I must admit the impossible has happened,' he said. '*Mon Dieu*: I would never have thought it. I think I have fallen in love. *Je te veux bien.*'

He turned to Isabel, unsmiling. Straightened her hat, lifted the veil. The lace pushed back, she now had an unobstructed view of his face, silvery green, with enquiring eyes.

At about four-thirty a.m. people began to go home. Punts set off alone at intervals, filled with loose-limbed revellers in stained and damaged clothes. When the last punt was about to leave, Jacques suggested he and Isabel should not take it, but walk back a little later. She agreed. She wanted the night to last, not for ever – people who expressed such views were thereby impeding the order of progress – but for a while yet.

So they were left behind. They stood on the bank, waving, the objects of much good-humoured speculation, till the punt rounded the bend, leaving only a few long, sleepy laughs and cries in its wash.

They stood in silence till the voices were finally no more, and then heard bright new laughter behind them. It was distinct, infectious. In the gunmetal light of the dawn sky, Isabel could see Jacques looked annoyed.

'So we're not the only ones, after all. Others are still here.'

He pushed his way through the branches of the willow tree. In a moment he was back.

'No one,' he said. 'I could have sworn I heard . . .'

'So did I.'

'Well, if there's no one, that's good. I wanted you alone.' He patted her shoulder. 'You're cold.'

'Not very.'

Jacques took off his blazer, put it round her.

'I feel,' he said, 'I don't know – restless. Stiff from all the sitting. Do you mind if I stretch my legs for a few yards? Back in ten minutes.'

'Of course.'

Isabel watched him walk away from her. He quickly disappeared into the mist that rose from the ground, a milk-grey mist that matched the paling of the sky.

The place, now everyone had gone, was lonely, the silence oppressive. Isabel longed for birdsong, the dawn chorus, the lowing of cows – anything to cloud the quiet into which the laughter might break again. She felt unsafe without Jacques at her side. Afraid. She wished she had her watch, so that she could time his return.

There it was again: the laughter.

This time it was nearer, but muffled. It was definitely coming from under the willow tree: people hiding, joking, trying to frighten her, was Isabel's immediate thought. Crossly, in her nervousness, she parted the branches and entered the hiding place. On the ground, the candles had burnt out in their jars. A blue suede sandal lay on its side, heel broken. But there was no one there.

Isabel heard herself utter a small cry, clap her hand to her mouth. She turned, ready to hurry outside, when a man appeared through the thickness of the branches.

'Jacques!' she screamed.

As she darted towards him, he backed away, indistinct in the poor light. But she clearly saw a flash of long white hand streaked with black mud, and a recognisable expression of something like evil. Then he was gone, vanished with no word. What terrible game was he playing? Isabel put a hand on the tree trunk to support herself. She was icy, shivering, confused. What had happened? What was this terrifying trick all about? Isabel looked round at the silent jangling shadows of the willow leaves, and knew she could not bear another moment in this horrible place. She must find Jacques, get him to explain . . .

She ran through the branches, hating their touch, and on to the tow-path. It was lighter now: that luminescent moment before real daylight. Isabel looked upriver. No sign of Jacques.

But, some twenty yards ahead, a girl. She was standing with her back to Isabel, looking in the same direction, upriver. Her presence brought relief. Obviously, she was a member of the party who had somehow missed a lift home.

Isabel called out to her. The girl did not move. In the silence between them, Isabel had the curious sensation that she was looking at herself, a mirror image, a reflection that she could not explain. The stranger on the path was the same height. She wore a long, bleached dress, though no detail was clear. Her hair was piled up in the same manner as Isabel's, though she wore no hat. Isabel put her hand to her head and found that her own hat, too, had gone. At the same moment, the reflection touched her hair. Isabel, remembering she had left the hat in the punt, shivered violently.

But, in her usual disciplined way, she called upon every source of common sense to come to her rescue. She was not a great believer in the supernatural: she had never seen a ghost. She did, however, acknowledge that strands of time can be confused, most particularly when some event of great significance has occurred. The complications of such theories were beyond her, and at this moment she gave them no thought. Curious, alarmed, she wondered what trick of the imagination, the light, her eyes, had caused this insubstantial vision of a girl who appeared to be a replica of herself. Perhaps, she thought, it was a mirage. Or even the unaccustomed quantity of pink champagne.

She called again.

This time the girl turned to her. For an infinitesimal moment she could see that she had no face – that is, no face delineated by its features. Instead, beneath the piled-up hair, was a simple disc, silvery transparent as the waning moon. In the second that Isabel was trying to re-adjust her focus, there was a loud crash, a hectic splash in the water. She swerved round to see that two swans had landed. They had set up their positions, cob following swan, in huge swirling necklaces of brown ripples. While the sudden noise had frightened her, the peaceful domesticity of the scene now reassured her. The swans were substantial, safe, not the stuff of illusion. She turned again to see what reaction they had caused in the girl. But she was no longer there.

Jacques was in her place, walking quickly towards Isabel. Happy, judging from his bouncing stride. Isabel ran to him. He waved. From a distance Isabel noticed his hand was streaked with mud. When she reached him, the hand was clean. There was no time for calculations.

Isabel flung herself into his arms. He held her.

'What's all this – hey? What's happened to the happy face of the girl I love?'

The face was buried in the concave chest, feeling the warm dampness of his cotton shirt. Jacques, confused, continued his teasing tone.

'I gave you ten minutes, precisely, to make up your mind. What were you thinking? Do you love me? Or is this heart to be unrequited?' He pushed Isabel away from him. 'Is it something serious? Tell me what's happened. Tell me as we walk back.'

Isabel could not be sure – she could not be sure of any-thing in this unnerving dawn – but she thought she detected a note of malice in Jacques' concern: the voice was hollow, somehow. Unsoft. Fighting such thoughts, fully aware of her confusion, she took his arm. Pressed together by the narrowness of the tow-path, they began the walk back to Oxford. Long grass each side of them was feathered with dew. Birds had begun to sing. In the secu-rity of near daylight, Isabel did her best to describe the hallucinations, knowing how ridiculous they sounded. Jacques made light of her experience – to comfort her, perhaps, she thought. He seemed untroubled, amused by her story: suggested someone could have spiked her drink. But he did agree that he, too, had heard unaccountable laughter.

By the time they arrived at Magdalen Bridge, the sun was up and busses passed to and fro.

'You must not give another thought to all the weird happenings,' Jacques said. 'I put them all down to an unac-customed drink, and much too much hard work. I'd say you're a little overwrought. You haven't had enough fun at Oxford so far. I mean to change all that. Now you must go back and get some sleep. When you wake, what I ask you to think about is . . . me.'

They parted with a chaste kiss. Isabel, never more grateful for the normality of daylight, hurried back to her room. Her immediate concern was to get rid of the dress. She tore it off, ripping fragile seams, stuffed it into a plastic bag and took it to a dustbin behind the kitchens. Too awake to go to bed, she then sat at her desk, her mind ablaze with a plan. It was only when details of this plan were finalised that she pondered on Jacques' declaration, tried to determine what it meant to her. But rational analysis was elusive, blotted out by image after image of a faceless girl and a terrifying man, both of them familiar.

That afternoon Isabel returned to the second-hand shop near the station. The owner well remembered the bundle of clothes from which Isabel had chosen the dress. They came from a friend, a Mrs Williams, whose husband was a retired lock keeper. She gave Isabel the address.

Two days later, work finished early, Isabel found the Williamses' cottage. It was four miles west of Oxford, an unpretentious detached building on a small lane that ran between two cornfields. The only other habitation in sight was the lock keeper's cottage, presumably where Mr Williams had lived before his retirement. Isabel was hot after the bicycle ride, sweating. She pushed stray wisps of hair under her straw hat, and walked up the cinder path between lavender, rosemary and white tulips.

A large man of about seventy answered the door: rolled-up sleeves, braces, a gardener's hands. He smiled.

'I wonder if you can help me,' Isabel began. She realised she had made no plans for an opening explanation. 'I recently bought a dress from a bundle of clothes you were selling in Oxford. I was interested to know if you could tell me something of its history.'

Mr Williams did not seem averse to the idea of the company of a stranger. He invited her in. 'The wife's just put the kettle on,' he said.

Isabel followed him into a small front room of large polished furniture. Everything was brown – wallpaper, bristling sofa, thick curtains, dull velvet cloth on the table, and the different tones of brown, all burnished by the sunlight, conveyed a low-watt life. How gloomy such a room would be in November, Isabel thought. It was stifling, airless. Windows all shut. She sat on a brown wooden chair at the table, where the only relief was a bowl of orange silk poppies. The wall in front of her was covered in sepia photographs of ancestors in brass frames.

'So what can I do for you?'

Mr Williams' braces were brown, his eyes were brown. Isabel repeated her interest in the dress. Mr Williams gave no indication he thought this an untoward request.

'Can't say I remember it, precisely, the one you describe. There was a whole big bundle – maybe the wife will know the one you mean. All I can tell you is they belonged to my grandmother, Ellen. She was a good woman but she was vain. Always buying herself pretty dresses. We got stacks of them up in the attic, selling them fast. It's quite fashionable, they say, all that sort of old stuff today. We get a good price.'

Mrs Williams came in with a tray of beige cups, tea and brown biscuits. Her husband let out a long sigh. Isabel's heart was beating uncomfortably fast. She felt faint from the lack of air.

'Can you remember a cream dress, Jean, in the last lot that went to Oxford?'

'With forget-me-nots,' added Isabel. 'Muslin. A frill at the hem.'

Mrs Williams poured tea. In the airlessness of the room, it seemed to Isabel, there was a certain reluctance in her action. Her mouth was grim.

'Can't say I can,' she said at last. 'She had so many dresses, much of a muchness.'

She passed a cup of tea to Isabel, then took one of the framed photographs from the wall. 'This is her,' she said. 'Ellen. And Jack.'

Isabel studied the photograph. It was so faded the figures were barely discernible, splattered by milky white splotches. But she could make out the small, thin shape of a woman in a long, tight-waisted dress: impossible to tell if it was *the* dress. Her face was featureless, bleached out, a void beneath her piled-up hair. Beside her stood a tall, thin man, one side of his face too faded to see – in the other, a single eye was fierce, the corner of the mouth turned down. He wore a cricketing blazer, the stripes reduced to almost invisible sepia and cream.

'Can't see much, can you?' said Mrs Williams, a shade of triumph in her voice.

'Funny thing,' said her husband, turning to Isabel and snapping his braces one after the other, 'but you quite put me in mind of Ellen, the pictures I've seen of her. She was pretty all right. Trim.'

'Don't tell me you can tell what folk look like from old snaps, John,' said Mrs Williams. She left the room, taking her cup of tea. Her sharpness made no discernible effect on Mr Williams.

'To tell the truth,' he said at last, 'they were an odd couple, my grandparents. Can't help you much about the particular dress, young lady, but I can tell you they were a very odd couple. Tragic, really.'

Isabel listened to the muffled tick of the brown wooden clock.

'Why?' she asked, still light-headed from the lack of oxygen in the room.

'I shouldn't say this, but she came to a nasty end.' He glanced towards the door, checked there was no sound from his wife. 'The family doesn't like it talked about, but I'll tell you, seeing as how you bought one of Ellen's dresses. It was like this, so my father told me. Young Ellen was a pretty girl, lots of young men keen to court her, but she liked to keep herself to herself. Along came this Jack fellow, a farm labourer. He was tall, thin, but not half strong: could earn more than any of them in overtime during harvest week. Something a bit queer about him, though: wanted to get into the academic world, be a porter at a college, know what I mean? Ideas above his station. But he was the one who changed her mind about going out with a fellow regular, if you under-stand me.

'They used to do their courting, Jack and Ellen, down

the riverbank, a mile or so from here. He was a strong punter, Jack. Used to take Ellen off in her party dresses, tie up by that big willow – you might know the one I mean – for a picnic and whatever – nothing wrong, I don't suppose, being those days. We've a photo of them somewhere, down there, taken by Jack's sister, my Great Aunt Agnes. Those were the hey-days, I suppose. Then it all went wrong once they were married. There are stories, but no one has the details.'

Mr Williams, even in his wife's absence, lowered his voice.

'Well, Ellen, she refuses Jack first time he proposes. She's quite adamant. She loves him but she doesn't want to be tied down in marriage. So Jack, he bides his time: asks her again. Again, no, says Ellen: she was an independent woman, my grandmother. "Well, I'm not going to give up," says Jack, and the third time he asks her she comes round. Says yes. So they marry and have the one son, my father. Jack stays on the land, no more talk of college work. He slacks off a bit, so the word goes, drinks a bit. Money gets tight. Ellen says she'll go out to work, get a job as a serving maid in one of the colleges. She does, too. Christ Church. That may have been the start of it, the trouble. We can't be sure, but there was a rumour. My father says he remembers as a boy overhearing a row between his parents; something about a steward who'd taken a fancy to Ellen. Maybe she fancied him back. Anyhow, things definitely weren't good at home. Jack was drinking heavily.

'One day, about this time of year, they leave my father

with the next-door neighbour, and go off for the day downriver on a punt. Maybe some kind of celebration – birthday or wedding anniversary. Maybe some sort of patch-up in the place they'd been so happy before they married. Next thing, Ellen's drowned, Jack's taken off for questioning. He swore it was an accident. They'd had a good day, he said, but admitted he'd had too much to drink. His story was they were bounding about in the punt and it had tipped up. Ellen fell over the side – funny story, that, when you think how heavy a punt is. Ellen gets trapped beneath it, can't swim, can she? And those long skirts. You can picture it, her struggle. Jack says he tries to save her, but then he's confused with drink, isn't he? Doesn't try bloody hard enough, is what the family think. He brings her body up, though, dumps it on the bank, gives her the kiss of life, and that's the last kiss he ever gives her. Big trial, all over the papers. People round here still remember the Williams case. Any rate, he gets off. Scot-free. Well, no witnesses, no evidence. Case over: my father gets adopted by a cousin, the lock keeper here: that's how I came into the job. He and Jack never speak again, and I was never allowed to set eyes on Jack. By all accounts he was a nasty piece of work behind the sweet talk, and the funny thing is, he *did* end up in a college. I forget which one, some job in the kitchens.' Mr Williams paused. 'So I can't help you more than that. That's the story of my grandmother Ellen. I bet your dress was pretty . . . she had an eye for nice things, my gran. Sad ending, really. Moral is, as my wife Jean says, you shouldn't say yes when you mean no, however hard you're pressed.'

Isabel left soon after the story ended, apologising for the length of her stay. His wife did not appear again, though Isabel could hear sounds from the kitchen. Outside, butterflies lay spread-eagled on the front path. Isabel guided her bicycle between them, the sun heavy on her bare arms. She began the long ride back to Oxford slowly, for the machine was old and cumbersome, and the warmth of the afternoon sapped her strength.

Jacques' declaration of love spurred a slight change in his pattern of invitations. No more teas at Browns were suggested but, the evening after Isabel's visit to Mr Williams, he invited her there for dinner. They ate gravadlax and ravioli and Jacques asked Isabel, in his naturally formal way, if she would now go out with him. Such were his feelings, he said, he could not imagine any week, any day, without her. He loved her.

Isabel did not answer for a long time. Then she said, 'I think we should just remain friends, nothing formal. For the time being, anyway.'

Jacques' mouth tightened and a wayward shadow ran over his face.

'I don't understand,' he said. 'I've been very careful to take things at your pace. Not to alarm you, not to ask you too soon for any kind of commitment.'

'I know you have, and I appreciate that. I'm afraid I can't explain my reluctance . . . It's just a feeling, an instinct, that you and I would be wrong.' She knew there was no possibility of trying to explain to Jacques the signs, the reasons, that caused her to hesitate to take up his offer. He would observe once again that she was crazed from too much work, and suffered from a fevered imagination.

Jacques laughed.

'While girls less conscientious than you are flayed by love affairs, two years hard study with no light relief has left you haunted by unreal things, visions, illusions fostered by an exhausted mind. The fact is, you're simply *tired*.'

Was that the truth of it?

He sounded arrogant in his conviction. He patted her hand.

'It's not that.' Isabel tried to be patient. 'Honestly. I'm sorry.'

Jacques laughed again, this time a shallow laugh.

'You may think you can get rid of me that easily,' he said. 'But I've waited a long time for the right girl. I'm not going to give up. What do you want – a proposal of marriage? I'd be happy with that. Would that convince you of my love? Will you marry me when you come down next year?'

Isabel, like someone drowning, watched the remembrances unfurl: their first meeting in New College gardens, their first picnic, so many pleasant teas at this very table, Jacques' admirable restraint that exactly matched her own. She pondered, too, on the realisation of her secret love for him, a love still undeclared. Was she a fool to resist, or should she take heed of the tragic Ellen and the strangely familiar Jack?

Jacques could not quite conceal his impatience. 'What is your answer?' he asked.

'The answer is no, Jacques,' she said at last. 'I can't marry you.'

Isabel was aware that the words, even as she said them, did not belong to her. Her refusal of his first proposal was merely an echo, a reflection in time.

Jacques smiled quickly, as if not to alarm her.

'I shall ask you again,' he said, as she knew he would.

To Re-Arrange

a Room

*R*obert woke first. He glanced at Lisa. Tawny hair, slightly troubled look, even in sleep. He wondered if, when Sarah was back this time tomorrow, the image of Lisa would remain imprinted on the pillow, superimposed on reality.

He knew she had had a disturbed night. She had cried after he had made love to her, and promised it would be the last time he would see her weeping. Then she had turned away from him, restless. After a while, she had said 'Robert?', very quietly, and he had feigned sleep. He was exhausted by their interminable arguments – some calm, some whipped into the slashing words of anguished souls – while they tried to resolve the predicament that had suddenly (suddenly?) appeared six months ago. He did not want to spend their last night in further pointless discussion. There was nothing more to say. It was the end.

'Robert? In exactly five minutes I shall get up.' Lisa managed a smile. Robert touched her cheek. He understood he had five minutes in which he could change his mind, explode their decision. If he pulled her towards him, she could stay for ever.

'Right,' he said.

He tried for a neutral tone – should have been easy

enough, a single word. But it acted upon her like a gunshot. In a second, she was leaping from the bed, cold air splicing the warm scattering of sheets. In one long, continuous movement, she pulled on her jeans and jersey, snapped her hair back into a band, produced her severe, efficient morning face.

'Packing up won't take me long,' she said.

In the huge room that was both their kitchen and sitting-room, Robert poured himself coffee, sat down at the table. Helping her was beyond him.

'There's plenty of time,' he said. In fact, there was not. Sarah had insisted on arriving at two.

'How much?' The depth of Lisa's desperation sang out in the short question. Robert could not tell her she must be finished in an hour, if he was to re-arrange the room before Sarah's arrival. He watched Lisa rip Indian shawls from the sofa. She had put them there the first week she moved in, to hide Sarah's 'hideous' brown corduroy cover. Robert had found them enchanting. When they made love on the sofa, which they often did, they could hear the tinkling of small silver bells sewn to the shawls' fringes.

Lisa flung them into an empty box, where they expired with a few muted chimes. She gathered cushions, brightly coloured, vaguely ethnic. Some were embroidered with squares of glass mirror, angry eyes in the light of the February morning. Lisa kept back one to hug to herself.

'Still smells of the sea,' she said.

They had stopped in an east coast seaside town. Waiting for a shower to pass, they had sheltered in a gift shop, found it among all the ugly things. When the sky cleared, and a white sun came out, they took it to the beach. They spread their macks on wet sand, laid their heads on the cushion and waited till the incoming tide reached their feet.

'Sea lingers,' said Robert. He could see tide marks on the silk. His hand was shaking.

Lisa stretched up for the picture above the fireplace: sentimental watercolour of Edinburgh Castle. They had come across it in a shop behind Princes Street – Robert had slipped out of his conference on World Pollution to join Lisa for lunch. Later that afternoon, silent in front of Van Gogh's turbulent *Olive Trees* in the National Gallery of Scotland, she had cried out that he had never told her he loved her. Robert, startled, though they were alone in the gallery, told her to keep her voice down.

'*Why*,' she had cried, no quieter, not caring. 'Why've you never told me?'

Robert knew his helpless shrug appeared callous. It wasn't the place to explain.

'When you know it's the truth, what need?' he offered.

'That's not good enough.'

'I'm not a man of declarations, you know that. I try to act what I feel.'

'Women need declarations. At least, I do.'

'God, you do. I'm sorry I fail you there.' He gave her his handkerchief, kissed her wet cheek. It had been her first accusation. Their first row. After that, he often observed she tried to contain herself. But she could not stop asking the question.

Eventually, he did bring himself to say the words, in response to the hundredth time of asking. But it was too late. It was no good. Obliging with a response was not the same as a spontaneous declaration, Lisa screamed, just when he thought she would be pleased. He began to lose patience. From that moment, the fragile structure of their affair began to flounder.

She was swiping things from the shelves – ornaments, jars, postcards from mutual friends – throwing them into an empty box, careless of their fate as china and glass clashed against the cardboard. Then it was books, her books. Gaps left in the shelves, boxes full. The room stripped of all her things. Unrecognisable. Robert looked about, horrified.

'What about them?' He glanced at the curtains. Lisa had made them herself, cream linen. She had spent many evenings, at the beginning, sewing – saving money, she said, as her machine buzzed away. When she hung them, a veil of summer sunlight filtered through the folds. At night, the moon diffused itself through the loose weave of the material, making the room a shadow-cave.

'Can't take them. Much too big for my flat. Burn them, why not? *Keep* them, even?' She laughed nastily. 'Can you help me with the boxes?'

Why had he not asked her to be his wife? Why could he not have faced the whole palaver of divorce, Sarah's anger, Sarah's hurt? And spent the rest of his life with this wild, brave, sweet creature whose love for him had never been in any doubt?

'Course I'll help you with the boxes.'

'Then I'll be gone.'

They loaded her small car. She faced him. Snapped off

the band from her hair so that it fell about like it did in the evenings. Thin legs parted, arms folded, defiant.

'I've left the snowdrops,' she said. 'She'll wonder about them, but that's not my problem. You could throw them away, too.'

Robert shrugged. He did not like to speak.

'Well: for three years – thanks.' Lisa shivered. 'At least I'm glad it's February. Most years, after February, things get better.' She gave a fractional smile. They kissed. She drove away.

Robert decided to do all that had to be done very fast. The short time to himself between the departure of his mistress and the return of his wife was inadequate for any internal adjustment. But Sarah had been insistent. (Years ago, he had loved her in her most adamant moods.) It was two o'clock or never, she said. Her lease on the rented flat was up, she had to be out. She had no intention of wandering the streets while her husband, apparently agreeable to her return, indulged in solitary reflection.

It was an awkward job, taking down Lisa's curtains. Robert stuffed them into plastic bags and hid them in the shed. Even more difficult was putting up the old ones. He shook them out, heaved them up the step ladder. Fat blue roses entwined with sour green leaves, clinging to orange trellis. How many evenings had Sarah sat in front of them, garish floral halo behind her, listing reasons why he was a useless husband?

They were in place at last. Terrible. Drawn back as far as they would go, their bunchiness further darkened the room. Robert found the lime and blue velvet cushions, so carefully matched in bad taste, which used to stand on the brown sofa. Sarah liked them to be on tiptoe, Robert remembered: on one point, so that they made diamond shapes against the back of the sofa. He tried. They fell over. He couldn't try again.

What else? The shelf above the fireplace looked naked. He reinstated his father-in-law's picture of a prim galleon on frilly sea. Remembered the candlesticks. Lisa had moved them to the table for *use*, she sensibly said. But had never cleaned them, so their pewter had turned to luminescent black. Robert dumped them at each end of the mantelpiece. He threw away the stumps of candles, finally burnt out last night. Searching for new ones, he came across the photograph. He looked at it. He and Sarah in Paris, late Fifties. Their first illicit weekend. Taken by a student who had joined them for a drink in a café. They had bought the whole film from him, given him a few francs besides.

'God,' Lisa had scoffed when she found it one day, 'your *clothes*. You looked old *then*.' She had tossed the photograph away, no questions, not interested. You look even older now, she meant. Twenty years older than her – and don't forget it. At the time of the photograph, he and Sarah had felt very young. The solemn handbag was no indication of passionate spirits. His love for her had been on a different plane . . . still was.

He remembered that the day Lisa had sneered at the photograph was the day he began to wonder.

It was all done by twelve. Robert sat in the armchair pushed *back* from the fireplace, as Sarah liked it. Shorn of its crumpled shawls, scraped down to the skin of its beige brocade, it felt skinned naked, alien. He would have to ask her for a few changes . . . above all, the curtains.

His hands and feet were frozen. This time last year it had snowed. Lisa and he had walked through the Savernake Forest, snow-quiet, muffled breaking of twigs, arguing about the power of the past – its habit of intrusion. Oh God, what have I done?

Into the silence bit the quiet, menacing crunch of his wife's key. She had refused to give it back – said it would be symbolic of giving up hope. He had thought it impolite to change the locks. She could be trusted not to come round.

He stood, turned. Sarah's eyes were crinkled into a wonderful smile. Perhaps she had just been out shopping, never been away.

'Everything's the same,' she said, looking round.

He saw at once in her ageing body and lively face the woman he had always loved most, despite everything. He went towards her, hoping, dreading. His own smile, un-expectedly easy, responded to her innocence.

They kissed. In the tangle of guilt about her, about Lisa, only one thought occurred: you could spin a whole axis in a single morning. To re-arrange a life, you simply had to re-arrange a room.

Sarah, drawing back from him, had observed the Paris photograph on the mantelpiece.

'My worst nightmare,' she said, 'was that you might have changed things. But you haven't. Once we've had the curtains cleaned, you'll never know I've been away.'

'May it be that easy,' Robert said. Her busy eyes had now reached the table, and Lisa's bowl of snowdrops.

Alternative

Behaviour

Where did we go wrong?

She'll stomp into the kitchen, Meriel, stub out her roll-up cigarette in a saucer though there's always an ashtray provided. She'll look in the fridge, slam shut its door with a snort of disapproval no matter how much it holds; she'll push back my cooking things and sit herself on the table and swing her skinny legs weighed down with those horrible great boots. Even before she's said a word, Meriel brings menace into the house. She shatters our peace. In truth, we're afraid of her.

What should we have done differently?

We've tossed the question between us so many times that it's become stale. We can find no solutions and we can't go on asking ourselves, says Douglas, quite rightly. We can't go on torturing ourselves, condemning ourselves, battering ourselves with guilt, exhausting ourselves with questions that have no answer. Our firm intention is just to accept, to question no more. But the haunting remains, the wondering. The constant regret.

Sometimes, when we slip into theories without meaning to, I suggest to Douglas it's because we're so dull. A dull, once happy couple. Reluctantly, he agrees. He doesn't like to think we're dull. To him – to me, we're not. Until all this, we have had and appreciated our small pleasures in life: security, just enough money, solid house with a nice bit of garden for the roses that are Douglas's hobby, holiday abroad most years, quietly in the same hotel near the Pyrenees where we can walk and gather wild flowers.

By others' standards, our ambitions have been minor ones and we feel no smugness in having achieved them to some extent – Doug a partner in the firm of solicitors after only twenty years. He specialises in divorce and never ceases to be amazed by other people's unhappy marriages. Over the years he's come back with stories of cruelty and violence and calculated unkindness you'd scarcely believe. But he enjoys the job. He's good at it, plainly. Also, his golf has improved as well as his roses – I doubt you'd see a better show of them anywhere in Berkshire.

As for me: well, all I've ever wanted was a quiet life, running the house efficiently, cooking for the family, enjoying the Bridge Club once a week. When Meriel went to weekly boarding school, I admit I did indulge in a few evening classes in pottery, History of Art and botany – things I'd had no chance to study at school and had always hankered after. But whenever Meriel was at home I'd put them to one side. I'd make sure my reading was finished by the time she was back so that I could listen to all her news over a slice of Victoria sponge, drive her over to her friend Lily – whatever she wanted. In all fairness, I don't think she could ever accuse me of neglect, though I suppose, yes, our life to her might seem unexciting. *Dead*, she called it, in one of her rages.

I had three miscarriages before Meriel. The nine months

of pregnancy with her I found hard to believe – hard to believe she wasn't one more life snuffed out before it had a chance. We had always wanted two children, but once Meriel was born, a perfect baby, we decided not to try our luck again. We felt it wouldn't be possible to love another child so much, and all desire to put the matter to the test dissolved. Meriel was enough for us.

'But we must be sure not to suffocate her with love,' I remember Doug saying. We tried very hard to be sensible parents – balanced, understanding but not spoiling, disciplining but not regimenting. We tried to inculcate in her from an early age a curiosity and love of simple things . . .

She'll barge into the house, drinking beer straight from the can and when she's finished it she'll crumple the can up in one hand as if it was so much tissue paper. She has big, manly hands, sinews tough as chains under the hard skin, flat fingers that pry over our things with distaste. Recently she's had her hair shaved round the back and a new earring at the top of her ear. Some years ago, she dyed her hair pink and had it standing up in points, like a clown. I managed not to say anything, and over this new shaved look I'm doing my best not to make any comment. But, I mean: Meriel's twenty-three now. She's no teenager. She's grown up.

By the age of five she knew the names of dozens of wild flowers and was an endearing, rewarding child. Not pretty, exactly: nose a little too prominent, like her father's – eyes a shade too close together, perhaps, but the bright blue that comes from my mother's side of the family. Everyone said she had lovely hair, and she was always turned out neatly – hand-smocked dresses and well-polished shoes. She was a bright little thing: happy, gregarious, loving. She would fling her arms around Doug's neck and ask him for an ice-cream or a story, knowing he would be unlikely to refuse her. From an early age, she would dedicate all her artwork to me, bright pictures of birds, and flowers bigger than the flat houses, *I love you Mum* written in the corner. One of her teachers assured us her draftsmanship was exceptional and she might well be an artist. I was inclined to agree.

At the age of nine, I think it was, Meriel began to show the first small signs of revolt. It was then we noticed that order, so much the norm in our house, seemed to frustrate her. No matter how much I tidied up her room, or per-suaded her to do so, it was only a matter of hours before neatness had given way to havoc. She seemed to get a charge from flinging things off shelves on to the floor, rum-maging through the neat piles of clothes in her drawers until they looked like a jumble sale, pulling her mattress on to the floor where, she said, she preferred to sleep. Her untidy ways weren't confined to her own room, either. In the kitchen, she spilt things so often it seemed clear it was on purpose. She threw her clothes all over the place, rum-pled the cushions, left books and papers on the floor. I think we both felt she was deliberately trying to annoy us, and took some pleasure in our discomfort and unease. Douglas and I hate things out of place: a sense of meticulous order has always been the staff we lean on.

By the time she was twelve, Meriel had given up at school. She was in constant trouble with her teachers and, apparently, no longer interested in any subject, even art.

No more paintings for me. Her father could no longer persuade her to read a book, any book. Her short attention span could accommodate no more than a teenage or music magazine. She spent most of her pocket money on these publications, then flung them down wherever she happened to be.

'Do pick up your magazine, Meriel.'

'Cool it, Mum.'

'Do as your mother says, Meriel.'

'For Christ's sake, stop nagging.'

'Don't adopt that tone with your mother, Meriel, or I shall stop your pocket money.'

'Go ahead and stop it. See if I care.'

'Meriel! Don't be so rude to your father.'

'Oh, piss off, both of you.'

Such language, at twelve. There were variations on this ritual exchange, then Meriel would clump out of the room, stomping the pages of the offending magazines to a mush on the floor in her utter scorn.

In the end, I would always be the one to clear them away.

It was about this time – just before Christmas, I remember – that Meriel chose to rebel against her name.

'What on earth was up with you, giving me such a daft middle-class name? You can imagine how *that* goes down at school.' Surely not too badly, I thought. The school was full of Virginias and Camillas and Emilys, a nice bunch of middle-class girls. 'You can't blame them for sneering,' she added, sloshing her tea aggressively over the side of her mug – a hideous mug, incidentally, orange decorated with black lettering: ***k You, mate*. When it was on the shelf, I always hid it behind another mug, turning the lettering away. Time and again I would find it placed back right in the front, its message staring my visitors in the face. It was one of our unspoken battles. Sometimes the mug so enraged me that I vowed I would throw it out, or break it on purpose. But I never went quite that far for fear of Meriel's revenge taking some even more drastic turn . . .

Douglas was concentrating on his *Daily Telegraph*, in one of his best-to-ignore-her moods.

'So anyway, from now on I'm not Meriel, I'm Mog.'

'Meg?' asked Doug, despite himself.

'Not Meg, no thanks. *Mog*.'

'Mog? But Meriel's a lovely name,' I ventured. We had agreed on it within moments of her birth. The small scrunched-up pink face *looked* like a Meriel, I remember saying to Douglas.

'Mog it is. I'm telling you – anyone who doesn't call me Mog won't get an answer. Meriel is *dead*.' She banged down her fist so hard that the Formica table skittered on its thin legs.

'We'll see about that,' said her father, in his most authoritative voice, which sometimes had effect.

'We will,' I agreed. 'Meriel. Mog, indeed!'

She won in the end, of course. Weeks went by when she responded to any question with persistent silence if we called her Meriel. *Mog*, eventually we said, in desperation. We were rewarded with a pleased smile. The triumph of a victory made her more agreeable for a while. And naturally we only called her Mog when we had to. If sometimes we slipped up and said Meriel by mistake, we were regaled with the old fury and rudeness. Our daughter hadn't an ounce of forgiveness in her.

We were prepared for a difficult time during Meriel's teens – that was to be expected. But we never imagined she would push our tolerance quite so far: pierced nose, shaven head, a tattoo on her shoulder – all done without our permission. As for her clothes – in a word, revolting. Why did she always want to make the *worst* of herself? That's what we couldn't understand. Our pretty daughter, at fifteen, was replaced by a brutish, alien creature we scarcely recognised. Drugs were our greatest fear, of course. They seemed the obvious next step. She was in with a bad lot. But when we ventured to have a conversation about the dangers – well, she just laughed, full of scorn. She'd never been into drugs, she said. *Demos* were more her thing.

Indeed, this seemed to be the case, as we discovered to our horror. Most weekends she'd go off with some renta-crowd – anti-students' cuts, anti-blood sports – it didn't seem to matter what it was, if there was a chance of joining a rowdy mob and throwing bricks at the police, Meriel would be there. You'll get arrested, we said. Who cares? she said. You must pay for what you believe in. We despaired. But there was nothing we could do.

Then came the day she walked in with a nasty cut above her eye. Didn't say a word. Dashed up to her room before I could offer to bathe it for her. Shut herself in her room. She wouldn't come down for supper, though she did ask for aspirin. When I asked if I could help, I was told to mind my own business.

After that, as far as we could tell, she went to no more demonstrations. But we noticed other changes. She began to grow her hair back. The fridge was no longer full of cans of beer. She seemed to go out less with her friends. She was working, she said, in her room: and we believed her. So in some ways she became a little easier, though her aggressive feminism and vegetarianism seemed more deeply entrenched than ever. As for her political correctness! We could hardly open our mouths without making some *faux pas* in her eyes. When Douglas complained that an Indian plumber had done a useless job, she threatened to report him for racism. When I said something about the Chairman of the WI, I was blasted with a ten-minute lecture on the necessity of addressing such a figure as a Chair*person*, even though the grey-haired old lady I had referred to had been happy as *Chairman* for the last twenty years. As for the food problem: while I tried my best to cook her things with vegetables and pulses, she sneered at us for our love of the Sunday joint which she, too, once used to enjoy, and our mid-week cottage pie. She managed to make us feel very uncomfortable at meals: always on about the cruelty of killing animals, the dangers of animal fat, and so on. Sometimes I could see Douglas was near to exploding, so goaded by her thoughts. But he managed to keep control, not to shout. It was hard for him just to let her have her say, unchallenged: but easier than the screaming row that would ensue if he tried to reason with her. *Reasoning* was the least of Meriel's abilities.

She did surprisingly well in her exams – no cause for celebration, she said when I baked her a cake she refused to eat because there was 'dangerous' colouring in the icing. Nothing very fancy about getting a few good marks, she said. Just meant it made her way into university that much easier.

Psychology was her subject. Psychology! Douglas raised his eyebrows, signalling only a fraction of the pain he felt. Couldn't she have chosen something better than a trendy, soft-option subject, he asked? With her brains – and he was proud of her brains – history: why not history? She'd done so well in that. Foolish man! He should have learned by then to keep his opinions to himself. Meriel went berserk, screaming at him, banging doors. 'What do you know about what motivates me? When have you ever cared about me as a *person*, not just as your daughter?' Then she slammed out of the house, leaving those cliché questions of modern jargon heavy between us, saying she was going to her friend for the night. (Boy or girl? We did not know). Douglas did not bring up the subject of psychology again.

Once Meriel had gone to university, the house became very quiet. Easier. We were aware of the luxury of peace, of no fear of tantrums or accusations. Surprisingly, she wrote to us several times – ordinary, newsy letters, telling us how she was doing, how she was enjoying university life. She had found a lot of people there who thought like her, she said. Like-minded, was the way she put it. (God forbid, said Douglas.) Once or twice, she even rang us – non-commital, but quite friendly. Then, her third term, we discovered Douglas had cancer.

For some time, he had been complaining about a painful shoulder. He thought it was rheumatism, or arthritis, per-haps. But as it did not improve over the weeks, he agreed to go to the doctor. He was X-rayed. A tumour was found. There were tests. Malignant, it was. A course of immediate chemotherapy was prescribed. I wrote to Meriel, breaking the news as gently as I could.

Twelve hours after receiving my letter she was home. Douglas and I were sitting by the fire with our hot drinks before going to bed, trying to make decisions calmly, in the way that people strive to in a crisis – what would happen about the business, and so on . . . Anyhow, Meriel comes barging in, giving us the fright of our lives. She's red-eyed, shouting, hysterical. Then she's all over her father, hugging him, crying. He has to push her away because, inadvertently, she hurts his shoulder. Then she sits on the floor, hugging her knees (which are poking out of torn jeans) and begins to spew out all this stuff against conventional medicine. The reason she has rushed home so fast, she says, is because she had to stop us deciding in favour of the treatment. Chemotherapy was crap, she said. Had we considered the side effects? Did we know how rarely it was successful? Conventional medicine was for the most part crap. The only way to certain recovery was *alternative*.

There was a long silence. Meriel was staring at her father's doubting face. She shuffled over to him, put an arm around his neck, more gently this time, leant her cheeks against his, just as she used to when she was a small child.

'Believe me, Dad,' she said. 'I've been studying all this sort of thing. It's all to do with positive attitude, freeing the body and soul from all the aggro that's been storing up so many years. Why do you think you've got cancer? Stress, that's why. You're stressed out, Dad.' She glanced at me.

I could see Douglas inwardly wincing at all those jargon words he hates so much, but at the same time he was touched by Meriel's unusual concern. This strange turn of events caught him off-balance. It was a moment, I could see him thinking, which he had to play carefully. If he said the wrong word, off she would stomp again, offended by the spurning of her advice and concern. If he agreed . . . what would we say to our doctor?

'For a start, you've got to get all the anger out of you,' Meriel went on after a while. 'It's got to be released.'

'But I'm not angry,' Douglas said.

'That's what you think. Listen, I know about these things, Dad. Honest, I'm a member of the Healing Society. I'm a Healer. I admit I haven't much experience, hands on, like. But I understand the principles. I believe in it one hundred per cent. When Mum wrote to me with the news, I couldn't help thinking here was a God-given chance to do something worthwhile at last. Make up for my – er, in the past.'

She put her hand on her father's knee, something she hadn't done for more years than I could remember. She looked very young, a child. Douglas seemed to be thinking the same thing. There was a brightness in his eye. He was close to tears.

'You're a good girl,' he said at last. 'I appreciate your concern. I'm not out of sympathy with all the alternative medicine bit myself, as a matter of fact. I've read quite a bit about it – I've been reading everything I can about ruddy cancer in the last few weeks, as you can imagine. But the fact is, this business—' he freed his hand from Meriel's, briefly touched his shoulder— 'could gather speed. I can't afford to hang about. I'd be a fool not to take the experts' advice, start the treatment. We're in very good hands, you know.'

Meriel moved a few feet away from her father. She looked at him with the hard eyes we were used to when she was not immediately able to get her way.

'Do this for me, Dad,' she said. 'Give me a chance. Just a few weeks. It's all a matter of diet, massage, positive thinking. Attitude is everything. Like: there are only another two weeks of term. I won't go back. I'll stay here, organising a programme for you. Starting tomorrow. I'll prepare your food, prepare your soul, Dad. Honest. In fact, not tomorrow – now. No time like the . . . We'll start with a massage, relax you, build up your confidence . . .'

Douglas's eyes moved about, alarmed. Again, he touched his shoulder.

'I'd rather not, a massage,' he said.

'I won't hurt you, stupid. It'll just be temples and toes. You've no idea how much good work on the toes can do.' She gave a confident smile. 'I'll explain it as I go. Now, you lie on the floor, Dad, nice and comfortable, cushion under your head. I'll just get my oils. Let's give it a go. All right?'

Douglas nodded, very weary.

'Very well,' he said.

Half an hour later, I could scarcely believe my own eyes. There was Douglas stretched out on our fluffy carpet, eyes shut, socks off. Meriel, kneeling beside him, was kneading at the furrows on his poor dear brow with her big flat thumbs. She would work them right up into his temples, where once the hair was thick and handsome, and was now so thin. There was an overpowering, claustrophobic smell of lavender oil in the room – a smell, I was later to learn, you can never quite extinguish from a room. A smell I came to associate with the terrible weeks of Meriel's 'cure'. Nothing like the summer smell of lavender bushes, or dried lavender in a muslin bag. In its concentrated form, it is menacing, sickening. I could see Douglas's nostrils twitch, affronted. But he said nothing. He kept his eyes shut, allowing his head to roll with her hands as she kept up a perpetual stream of theories. 'Trouble with you, Dad, is you're suffering from a crisis of identities.'

'I don't think your father is doing any such thing,' I heard myself saying.

'You don't know anything, Mum. That's been one of Dad's problems.'

She moved down to his feet. Watching her at work on them was even more upsetting. The private nature of feet came home to me: no wonder people don't want them exposed. They are not the most attractive part of anyone's body. Douglas's were long and thin, sinewy. The white ridges of bone that stuck up put me in mind of a plucked chicken's wings. As for the nails, well, even the most loving wife would have to admit they were not a pretty sight. Wide, flat, lobster-coloured nails, Douglas had, each one topped with an arc of dense yellow that curved cruelly into the hard flesh of the toes. Sometimes they caused him pain and he would have to go to the chiropodist, who said he had a problem. All this I was familiar with – part of my husband, for better, for worse – a huge blessing he wasn't one of those men who liked to wear open sandals. But it didn't seem right to me, a daughter on familiar terms with her father's feet. There she was, pulling at each toe, prying into the secret places between them, all the time droning on about how each toe sent signals up to wherever. Sounded like a lot of stuff and nonsense to me, but I knew I had to go along with Douglas, do whatever he wanted.

When at last she had finished, Douglas sat up very fast, giving the sudden appearance of a fit man. But he looked dizzied, confused. Meriel sat back on her heels, very pleased with herself. She stretched out her hand, held it a few inches from her father's chest.

'There: I can, like, feel the energy coming off you already, Dad,' she said. 'The anger – can't you feel? It's beginning to make its way out.'

Douglas gave her the faintest smile, patted her on the head. He looked so . . . what was it he looked? I couldn't put a name to it for a moment. Then I suddenly knew what it was: *undignified*. That was it. For the first time I could ever remember, my husband's dignity had been ripped from him. He sat hunched on the floor, oily bare feet ashamed in the fluffy pile of the carpet. His thin hair darkened by the lavender oil, and all askew.

'Go on, tell me you don't feel a difference.'

Meriel gently stroked his feet with a possessive intimacy that gave me the creeps.

'Can't say I feel any benefit *yet*,' he said carefully, 'but then it's early days.' He gave Meriel another smile. She put her arms around his neck. 'Oh my dear, dear girl,' he said, with a kind of exhausted relief, as if this physical contact with his daughter was something he had been hoping for for a very long time.

Upstairs, Douglas had a bath and washed his hair. But nothing would get rid of the smell of the lavender. It came off his skin like some terrible incense, increasing the discomfort of our argument – whether we should agree with Meriel's well-meaning but useless theories – that went on till dawn began to light the familiar things of our room, and the day threatened.

But having lost my argument, I did my best when it came to a show of solidarity. I wore my new red coat, and the gloves Douglas had given me at Christmas, for our visit to the specialist. Douglas put his thoughts to the man with all the articulacy he was capable of when addressing a difficult client. You'd think he'd been an advocate of alternative medicine for years, the way he described the reasons for his decision. He was determined to give it a try, he said. A man had to have faith in his daughter. The specialist listened politely, a sceptical frown on his brow. Then suddenly he shrugged his shoulders, almost as if he thought there was no point wasting precious time on one so obdurate as Douglas, and suggested a compromise. Why not *go along* with Meriel's ideas, he said – after all (and here he allowed himself a small chuckle) they could not do much positive harm. Why not start the course of treatment right away as well? There was a small silence while Douglas considered this reasonable proposal. The specialist looked at his watch.

'In cases like yours, there's no time to be lost,' he said.

With this piece of news, Douglas made up his mind instantly.

'No,' he said. 'I'll give my daughter a chance first. Just for a few weeks.'

'Very well,' said the specialist, and saw us out into the stuffy corridor. I felt as if our lifeline had been snapped. But I kept my fears to myself, and drove Douglas to his office. He was to start arrangements for his deputy to be in charge. Although he intended still to work some days a week, already it was apparent he was not up to a full week in the office. Fatigue hit him every day after lunch. This afternoon, however, he seemed to be full of beans. I secretly wondered, only for a moment, whether there might be something in Meriel's gobbledy-gook after all – some magic, some transference of will. I don't know. I do believe miracles can happen. Though nothing could convince me Meriel could be the perpetrator of the sort of miracle we needed.

I got home late that afternoon, having been shopping at Sainsbury's. I got home to find that Meriel had already been on a spending spree of her own. The kitchen table was entirely covered with fruit, vegetables, and several blue glass bottles of essential oils and many packets of vitamins. In an expensive-looking new liquidiser she was making raw carrot juice – I refrained from asking, but imagine Douglas must have lent her his credit card, or given her cash. A pile of chopped liver with a nasty bluish-purple shine lay on a board. On top of the fridge, propped up in the rude mug, a joss stick was burning. Its sickly smoke curled down over us. The blinds at the kitchen window were half-drawn. Meriel's portable CD player was on the draining board, Indian music mewing forth.

'What's all this?' I asked, lowering my own bags of provisions to the floor.

'Day one of Dad's diet. Starting with supper. Don't put on that face, Mum. Give me some credit.'

Did I put on that face again at supper? I hoped not. But as I watched Douglas struggle with a plateful of raw liver mixed with grated carrot, I could not be sure. Later, Meriel insisted on more pulling of his toes, though she did agree to a scentless oil. I could not bring myself to watch this revolting performance again. I went up early to bed and wept into the pillow.

'Please see some sense, Douglas, and stop all this nonsense. There's no time to lose,' I said, when at last, exhausted, he joined me.

He made an effort to be consoling. He promised me that if Meriel's methods did not result in definite improvements quite soon, he would return to the specialist.

'Don't you see,' he said, 'that she's come to make amends. If we reject her now, we'll lose her for good. As it is, she's back to loving us, wanting us, needing to do something very important for us. It would be madness to reject her. She'd be gone for good. We must give her a chance, whatever the cost.'

What could I do but nod, agree? Whatever feelings a wife may have, she must not add to her ill husband's problems.

In the middle of the night, I heard Douglas get up and go to the bathroom. He was there a long time, terribly sick. I pretended to be asleep.

*

The days go by slowly. Fraught. She'll stomp into the kitchen, Meriel, with bags of fruits and vegetables, pulses and grains and vitamins. There hasn't been any meat in the house – apart from the raw liver – since she came back. Not a thing I fancy, and I can't very well bake a batch of scones just for myself. Never a 'Anything *you'd* like, Mum?' What's more, she's taken over. She's in charge of what goes on in the kitchen. All I'm left with is the clearing up. Still, I suppose I can't complain. She's here, she's all over her father, paying him more attention than she has done for years. Almost an obsessive attention, I might add, as if it's important to her to make her point, to prove her alternative methods are right, superior.

She comes down late – never an early riser. So I do the breakfast, eating half a grapefruit to keep Douglas company, though I can't take the carrot juice. Douglas says its not bad, once you're used to it. He's been a hero, forcing himself to get used to Meriel's diet, I'll say that. Nowadays he only goes to the office twice a week – Meriel packs him a salad and fresh orange juice the night before – and comes back looking ashy in the evenings. But quite cheerful. 'Don't you think Dad's looking better, Mum?' Meriel keeps asking. I can see in his eyes Douglas is hoping for an encouraging answer. So, yes, I say, I believe he is. That's not the truth, of course. I keep the truth from both of them. My private opinion is that he's a bad colour –yellowy skin, a jaundiced colour. Also, he's lost a lot of weight very quickly. Half a stone in a couple of weeks, I'd guess. But that's not surprising, considering the rabbit food Meriel insists he eat. And when he's in her presence, I'm bound to admit he puts on a show of good spirits, swears he's feeling better. That pleases her. She kisses the top of his head and pats him with her big hands. I hate her at those moments. I believe I really hate her.

Evenings, there's a routine. After supper, she and Douglas go next door for another massage session. I really can't abide to watch. They're back on the lavender oil, now: as far as I'm concerned, the sitting room has become un-inhabitable. It stinks. So, after supper, I sit in the kitchen with biscuits and tea – Meriel's vegetarian concoctions aren't exactly filling, and of course I won't touch the raw liver – watching the telly. Every night Meriel tells me, at the end of the session, they're getting somewhere. An inner peace is replacing the old stress, she says. I look at Douglas, but he won't meet my eye.

One night it's one-thirty and they're still in there. I know Douglas needs to go to bed, it's his office day tomorrow. So I tap on the door, poke my head round. Well, it's really spooky. There's dreadful Indian whining music, the smell of joss sticks curdling with the stench of lavender oil. Douglas is laid out on the fluffy carpet, bare yellow feet poking out of the end of his trousers, hands of paler yellow spread out on his thighs, eyes shut. The flesh of his face, was my immediate thought, did not seem to belong to the same man. It was a terrible colour, a sort of thin grey, like the flesh of a snail.

Meriel, kneeling behind him, looks up. Her fingers are twirling about in the air above his chest, as if she is kneading invisible pastry.

'What do you want?' The usual aggression.

'I think it's time for your father to come up to bed.'

Meriel went on with her twirling, as if I had not spoken.

'Here, look at this, Mum,' she said at last. 'You can see what's happening, can't you? The core of his anger. You can see it coming out. It's like smoke, isn't it? It's tangible. You can *feel* it.' She pinched her finger and thumb together as if she was pinching snuff. It struck me she was completely mad. 'Once Dad's free of all this, he'll be well on his way to recovery. Cancer's, like, one hundred per cent caused by stress, anger, rotten feelings that fester into a kind of garbage inside you.' Her chant was familiar by now.

'Not one hundred per cent,' I ventured.

'Listen, I've studied all this. I know what I'm talking about.'

A matter of opinion, my girl, I said to myself. You've only been an undergraduate for under two terms, and you're meant to be studying psychology.

But there again, perhaps all this sort of talk *is* psychology . . .?

Douglas opened his eyes and struggled to get up. He looked very tired, but managed a smile. Both Meriel and I put out a hand to help him up. He had taken off his jacket. I noticed that beneath his shirt his shoulder bones stuck out like wings.

'Thank you, love,' he said to Meriel and I felt myself stung by a terrible feeling. The pain in my chest, the jealousy, was tangible. Then, perhaps aware of my feelings, he put his arm around *my* shoulders, thank God, and leant on me all the way upstairs.

Meriel went back to university at last. Never have I been so relieved. I opened the sitting-room windows wide to try to banish the smell of lavender oil, then set about clearing up my kitchen. She'd left instructions everywhere – pinned to the walls, stuck to the fridge: lists of ingredients I was to buy, how to make a lemon dressing, the importance of carrot juice at all times . . . I don't know. It wearied my head, trying to follow it all. I knew I'd never manage: my heart wasn't in it. In my opinion, what Douglas needed was some nourishing food, something to keep his strength up. I felt like ripping all the bossy little instructions down, throwing them away. Then I thought, better not. Not till I see what Douglas feels. He may want to keep the whole ludicrous routine going. Keep on giving it a chance. Besides, Meriel had left with so many threats. 'If you don't continue the cure scrupulously,' she had said, 'it will be your fault if Dad declines. As you can see, he's *much better* since I've been working on him. He's a different man. Can't wait to get back and tell the Healers about my success.'

I made a small batch of scones that day, put two or three on a plate for tea. When Douglas came home – he comes back much earlier now from his two days at the office – he took one, ate it slowly, relishing every bite.

'Guilty?' I asked with what I hoped was a mischievous smile.

'Just very hungry,' he said.

'What if I made you a steak and kidney pie for supper?'

'I'd eat it,' he said. Well, we hadn't had such a happy evening for weeks.

Douglas made some effort to return to carrot juice and so on for a couple of days, but we both agreed it was time for the experiment to come to an end. It was quite obvious there was no improvement in his condition: in fact, the truth was, as he admitted within a week of Meriel's departure, he felt bloody awful. No energy, much worse pain in his shoulder.

'But no need to worry,' he said. 'Mr Belton was so optimistic, remember? Said I'd probably got a few years, and quite a high chance of full recovery.'

'But you wouldn't start the treatment when he suggested it.'

'Won't have made much difference, six or seven weeks. All the same, I'd like to go back and see him.' I could tell, by that, he was worried. We were sitting on the sofa. It was an overcast afternoon. He'd laid one of his thin hands on my knee. It quivered.

'*Why*, Douglas?' I asked. 'I'll never understand why you agreed to go along with Meriel's daft theories.'

'Surely you should understand,' he said, so gently. 'I had to win her back. We had to win her back. There've been so many years of alienation. I thought this might be the last chance. I thought it couldn't hurt. Might even be something in it.'

'You mean, you didn't believe in it all, although you kept telling her you did?'

Douglas shrugged.

'I couldn't disappoint her, could I? Here she was, with something *she* really believed in. I haven't seen her so enthusiastic, so involved in something, since she was quite a small child. Besides, I think she was trying to say sorry. Trying to make up for all the difficult years. I wouldn't have had the heart to reject that. You wouldn't, either.'

'She didn't like *me* any better, I noted.'

'One thing at a time. She's not capable of taking on several things at once, remember. She'll come round to you.' This was no time to argue.

'So what do we do about telling her, Doug? About giving up her plan?'

He thought about it for a long time, in silence.

'We don't tell her,' he said at last.

The following week we returned to Mr Belton, the specialist. He interviewed Douglas at length. It was hard to read his thoughts, but I fancied he looked concerned. Douglas, he said, had lost a stone.

'I thought it was worth giving it a go,' Douglas said.

'It was up to you,' Mr Belton said – not unfriendly, exactly. More, a little impatient. He made an appointment for more tests, X-rays. A few days later, Douglas left his office for good. Meriel rang up most evenings.

'How's the routine going?' she kept asking. 'Carrot juice three times a day? You must be getting used to chopping up the raw liver by now, Mum.' We lied to her. We lied and lied, bright voices. She was full of smug pleasure, of course. The story about her father responding so well had been received with much interest, she said. These conversations were very trying. Each time Douglas put down the telephone he looked like a slain man.

'I'd give the world not to be doing this,' he said.

'Let's hope it's not one more of our mistakes,' I said. 'Dear God, where did we go wrong?' The question slipped out before I could stop it.

'We'll never know,' said Douglas.

*

149

Mr Belton summoned us to tell us about the results of the tests. This time, there's no denying he looked grave. One glance at his face and I knew what the news was going to be.

'The one thing that's certain about this disease,' he said, rubbing his healthy brown hands together, 'is its unpredictability. Sometimes, when all the signs have given little hope, it suddenly becomes almost dormant. Other times, you're pretty sure the patient has months, if not a few years, left, and the tumours multiply with a devastating speed.' He paused. 'I wish you hadn't postponed the treatment,' he said. 'But we'll see what you can do.'

He described it all to us in great and kindly detail, but his words were far away, blowing down through a thin tube in my ears that made an echo. On the way out, Douglas took my arm. I felt its terrible thinness. I felt the sinews tremble, but he was being so cheerful.

'Don't worry,' he said, 'I'm going to lick this thing. I'm a fit man, and whatever Meriel might think, not an angry one.'

We laughed, standing there in the car park, the cars a paintbox of colours flowing into one another. It was the last time I can remember we laughed, and Douglas asked me to drive.

It all gathered such speed after that, there was scarcely a moment to get back to this journal. Besides, I couldn't. I couldn't bring myself to describe the horror of Doug's fast decline: the small spasms of hope always quickly dashed by despair. I looked after him myself for as long as I could, then a nurse came in to give me some relief. His hair fell out. I became fascinated by a small pulse in his temple, beating away, roped in by a swollen blue vein, fat as a worm. Had they always been there, pulse and vein, beneath his hair, all the years of our marriage? It was the sort of thing I began to concentrate on, trying to deflect my thoughts from the reality of the situation. Douglas was dreadfully sick, and new pains began. Terrible stomach pains. It was time for all possible help, things beyond me. He agreed to go into the local hospice, a sunny place with windows on to a nice garden.

The time had come, too, to tell Meriel. I dreaded the call so much. In fact, I gave way to cowardice and wrote to her. I said the switch to conventional medicine had been a mutual decision. It was what Douglas wanted, what we thought would be best. I put it all as gently as I could.

Her first response was at midnight, waking me from a light sleep. A great spewing forth of abuse, anger, tears – all just as I had expected, only worse. Vitriolic. Accusing me of breaking her trust, betraying her. What sort of a mother am I, she asks. What sort of a wife? Giving up *her* way – so successful in just a few weeks, as we had all witnessed – and subjecting Doug to chemotherapy was tantamount to sticking a knife through his heart. When I tried to remonstrate, ask her to listen to reason, she just slammed down the telephone.

She kept on ringing. Whenever I came back from visiting Douglas – and I couldn't worry him with all this, of course – she was on the telephone with her horrible accusations.

This morning was the worst of all. So vicious I can only hope it was the last time she'll ring.

She accused me of killing her father.

'If we hadn't wasted weeks on your stupid methods, your father might not be lying there dying right now,' I shouted back. I was suddenly angrier than I'd ever been in my life, with anyone.

'You bitch,' she screamed. 'Bitch, bitch, bitch.' She disowned me as a mother, she said. I wouldn't see her again, not even at the funeral.

It's late at night now, but I've calmed down a bit. I try to put Meriel from my mind, concentrate only on Douglas. He was very tired this evening, weak. But cheerful as always, holding my hand. He doesn't ask about Meriel any more. He hasn't the strength to hear about disputes. He knows there's only a short time left.

Well, I'm not going to write my journal again after tonight. It's been cathartic in some ways, but nothing can help any more. Besides, I want to spend every moment from now on at Douglas's bedside. Often, sitting there, so quiet, I long to ask him one last time, where did we go wrong? But the time's past. Such a question would be an unfair burden in his pitiful state. Besides, the closeness of death rarely enlightens. Like me, he can have no answers.

The Wife Trap

Seventeen years after their divorce, Peggy Jarrett received a Christmas card from her ex-husband George. She had recognised his writing on the envelope at once, and was puzzled. There had been no word of communication ever since their apathetic farewell in Court, a sleety morning all that time ago. What was he up to now?

Nothing, it seemed. Peggy read the message several times.

Why don't you drop in for a cuppa if ever you're passing this way? Yours ever, George.

Whatever made him think she'd be his way? She had no reason to pass through Lincolnshire, some hundred miles north-east from where she lived. What a daft idea! Besides, in the unlikely event of her being in his direction, what would be the point of dropping in on a man with whom she had had seven years of nothing but boredom, irritation and disappointment? As a husband, George had been nowhere near up to scratch, in Peggy's mind, and she hadn't missed him once since their parting. Indeed, she'd scarcely given him a thought.

Nonetheless, she searched the card for clues. She held it up to the opal wintry light that hung flatly across her small kitchen window, her lips puckered in critical contemplation.

It was a traditional scene: coach and four in front of an olde inn, swirling snowstorm blurring the artist's incompetent draftsmanship. Rubbing her finger over the picture, Peggy could feel the raised paper that had been employed to depict the snow – a porridgy feel that made her shudder. A very low-grade card, she was bound to admit. But then George had never had her instinct for nice things. That had been one of the many life-dividers between them. His obliviousness of quality stuff – curtains, pictures, shoes, ties, anything you could mention – was one of the things that had driven her to despair. What's more, he had shown no inclination to *learn*. Things were just things, as he so often used to say, and as long as they functioned properly that was good enough for him. What do I care if a glass comes free from a garage or for twenty quid from bloody Harrods? he once asked. Funny how she remembered the question. He'd been standing in the kitchen clutching a tin of Quality Street to his stomach at the time. She could hear his sneery voice as if he were shouting at her this very moment. The Christmas card brought it all back to her, the remembrance of all the troubles she'd had with George; the fact that she had married beneath her, and regretted her mistake from day one of the honeymoon.

For a moment, Peggy wondered whether to throw out the card. But then she decided to put it with the rest, in a shoebox on whose lid she had written *Christmas 1995*. Might as well. She had quite a hoard of boxes now, proof that she was in so many friends' thoughts at the festive season. The presence of these cards was a peculiar comfort. Sometimes, even in the heat of July, she would take them out to recount them, and reread the messages of goodwill and cheer. Not that even Jen, her best friend and neighbour, knew anything of this secret ritual. Jen was a great one for Understanding Most Things, as she often reassured Peggy: but instinct told Peggy that there were some things that should not be confided even to a best friend, for fear of misinterpretation.

When she had put the card in the box with the rest of her collection, Peggy almost forgot about it. Although, during the course of the next eight months, her mind did occasionally turn, curiously . . . Once, years ago, she had found a dormouse curled up under a floorboard in deep sleep. She had not disturbed it, but remembering its presence every so often caused a small wick of comfort to flutter in her stomach. George's card acted in the same way.

In August, Peggy's sister Lil suggested Peggy go up for a week to see the new house she and Jack had bought in Alnwick. Peggy didn't much fancy the idea, and knew from experience a week with Lil and Jack would be more like hard work than a holiday. She was driven to distraction by Jack's non-stop boasting about how he was a man for a bargain if ever there was one. In their last tacky little house there was not a single item that had not been a bargain, it was too plain to see. Peggy held no hopes that the knock-down terraced house in Alnwick would be any different. She hated Lil's scarcely disguised sympathy for her own single life – sympathy! That was the last thing she needed, considering her own superiority of judgement was of quite a different class to Lil's; and then the children. They were the sort of children who made Peggy feel glad she had none of her own. Still, despite everything against the idea, Peggy decided she would go, just for a few days.

The visit passed just as she imagined it would, and on the journey home Peggy was aware of an unaccountable weariness. The thought of home, and peace, was cheering, but not all that cheering. As she sat in a motorway café eating her lunch, she reflected on the year ahead of unchanging routine: part-time job at Oxfam, the bridge club, choir practice once a week and dear Jen's interminable visits and enquiries. Nothing to complain about, but nothing to lift her spirits, either. For want of something better to do, she studied the map, thinking that a different way home might relieve the tedium of the next few hours. It was then, by chance, she noticed the small town where George lived, and remembered his card. She measured the distance from her present position with her thumb: some thirty miles, she reckoned. A short visit – cup of tea, exchange of awkward pleasantries – would be under an hour out of her way.

Peggy took but a moment to make up her mind. However unexciting the reunion might be, at least she could make it into a good story for Jen, whose own life always seemed so much more exciting than Peggy's.

An hour and a half later she drew up at an undistinguished house in a suburban street: neat privet hedges and a newly painted wooden gate. She walked up the straight little path feeling nothing at all, and rang the bell. After no response to three rings, she took the liberty of finding her way round to the back of the house. She saw George at the end of a long, narrow garden. The familiarity of his stance – he had his back to her – caused a strange constriction in her chest. He stood there, same as ever, legs apart like a Colossus of suburbia, hosepipe in hands, playing its jet of pale water over a bed of brilliant flowers.

George had worked all his life for a horticultural firm which sold packets of seeds by the million. It had always been his habit to avail himself of free packets, and to furnish the garden so that it looked like pages from the firm's glossy mail order brochures. All too vulgar for Peggy's taste, of course: always had been. Though she had seen the point of free flowers, and in this one matter had conceded to George's determination never to pay for anything in the garden.

She stood quite still, knowing she would have a moment or two to take in his unchanging shape before he turned and saw her. He wore slouching trousers of indeterminate beige, and a polo shirt of a particularly nasty rust that she, Peggy, would never have agreed to. His hair was perhaps a little thinner, and the neat side wings, that curved same as always over his ears, were greying. Had she seen enough? Was this a mad idea? Should she turn and run?

Even as these questions fizzed through her mind, Peggy saw that it was too late. George had spun round and was looking straight at her. He frowned for no more than a second – possibly the strong evening sun was in his eyes. Then he smiled and moved towards her, the water from the hosepipe at his side making a sloppy track across the lawn. He stopped a yard from her – deeper runnels in his cheeks, grey eyebrows, teeth he still had not bothered to have straightened – still smiling.

'Well, I'm blessed, Peg o' my life, I was just about to suss out the hydrangeas,' he said.

The years shot away from Peggy. His news had always been about gardening. Now, after a such a long absence, all he could think to greet her with was his own immediate plan concerning the hydrangeas.

'Were you passing?' he asked after a pause.

'More or less.'

'I knew you would. One day.'

Cocky bastard. All the same, Peggy smiled nicely. 'You've got quite a garden,' she said.

'Not a bad little patch. You should've seen it when I came here. Cup of tea?'

'I wouldn't mind.'

She followed him to the back door. He stopped to turn off the outside tap on the way, and kicked viciously at the green plastic snake of the hose. Once, he had kicked the cat, Pinky, so hard that he had caused a rupture. Peggy remembered Pinky as she looked about George's kitchen: a beautiful marmalade, lovely temperament, everyone said. There wouldn't be any animals here, of course. George loathed animals. Pinky was one of the many things that had come between them.

The kitchen was a room that personified George's view of his surroundings: functional. The walls were a nasty green. There were plastic blinds at the window, a torn shade on the overhead light, a Formica table patterned with ribbons and roses of crude yellow and blue. The smell of stale smoke reminded Peggy of another division of opinion between them, as did the full ashtrays. She had eventually trained George not to smoke in the kitchen, but obviously that rule had lapsed with his freedom.

Peggy drew her angora cardigan tightly round her, and sat on an uncomfortable stool at the table. George, whistling under his breath, switched on the kettle and dumped two mugs on the table. One of them, a souvenir of the Queen's Silver Jubilee, she recognised as theirs. The other was new and ugly. But then in the sharing of things, Peggy remembered, George had been quite generous, allowing Peggy her pick and saying he would not need much stuff just for himself.

Eventually George sat at the other side of the table. A tin pot of tea and a bottle of milk stood between them. Peggy felt some old habit rumbling up through her veins: without asking, she poured the tea. George's first.

'Well, well,' he said. 'What brings you to this part of the world?'

'I've been staying with Jack and Lil. They've got a new place up in Alnwick.'

'Ah, Lil.' George had never shown much affection for his sister-in-law, though once, at a Christmas party, Peggy had found him giving her more than just a polite kiss under the mistletoe.

'You've got a nice place up here, I must say. Very quiet,' she said. Might as well be friendly.

'Quiet! Don't you believe it.' George banged his fist on the table, making the tin pot shudder. 'It's wicked. Break-ins, burglaries, rape, mugging, the lot. Terrible. I organised a local neighbourhood watch, as a matter of fact. I'm what they call the chairman. I'd say things have improved a bit since we put the notices up, but not much. You can't be too careful. Had to spend a fortune on security, I can tell you.'

Peggy followed his glance towards expensive locks on the windows and huge bolts on the door. He'd always had a thing about security, she remembered. But the precautions he had taken here seemed to her a little out of proportion to the value of the contents of the house. No burglar in his right mind would want anything from this kitchen, surely.

'You lock yourself in all right, do you?' George asked.

'Oh, I take good care.'

'Sometimes I've thought, you know – funny thing, but there it is – I've thought, come along, George, send a card to Peg o' my life and tell her to be sure to check her locks. It's a violent world today. But of course I never did. You know me, not much of a writer. So then I sent the Christmas card and lo and behold here you are, so I can warn you in the flesh.'

He smiled. But there was a look in his eye that was new to Peggy. A sort of flinty, manic glare. Possibly it was her imagination. The sun had tinged everything with a glowering orange, making Peggy unsure of her original impression. Perhaps George had changed, in some way she could not put her finger on, which aroused both unease and something vaguely exciting.

They chattered on about the hydrangeas, and George's plans for a new greenhouse, and his addiction to snooker on the television. Two pots of tea were drunk, and then they turned to cans of shandy. These lived on the ledge above the sink and were warm from a long day in the sun:

funny old George, still not much good at looking after himself. Never did remember to put drinks in the fridge.

Some time after eight (amazed, she was, how the time had flown) Peggy remembered the three-hour journey ahead, and said she had better be on her way. The three cans of shandy had made the roses on the table tremble as if through a heat haze. Still, she stood up quite firmly and announced her intention to leave.

'Oh, you don't have to go, surely,' said George. 'You can't drive till all the shandies have settled. It would be irresponsible to let you go. Sit yourself down and I'll get us a sandwich.'

Peggy let herself sink back on to the stool, whose seat had made grooves in her thighs. Suddenly exhilarated by a feeling that time did not matter, she made no protest. With incredulous eyes (in the old days George had never lifted a finger in the kitchen) she watched him open a tin of salmon, spread vegetarian margarine on sliced bread and cut up two homegrown tomatoes.

'Not exactly a feast,' said George, 'but there's plenty of raspberry ripple for afters, and I can probably lay my hands on a bit of cheddar.'

By now Peggy was hungry as well as tired. She ate gratefully, and found herself accepting a glass of homemade elderberry wine. They talked more about the greenhouse, and about who had been promoted in the seed firm in the intervening years (George mentioned a lot of names new to Peggy) and no mention of her own life was made. After they had eaten, they went to the front room – forlornly brown – and sat side by side on the old G-plan sofa that

Peggy, at the time of their parting, had said she would not miss at all. They watched the news, and the snooker, and by the time they turned it off a thin summery darkness had gathered outside the windows.

'Time to be turning in,' said George, as he had said every night of their marriage. 'Have to get up early. Why don't you stay the night, Peg o' my life? It's a bit late to start back now. I've got a perfectly good spare room: never been slept in, as a matter of fact.'

Peggy stifled a yawn. He was quite right, of course: it was no time of night to be setting off cross-country. She sat for a while in easy silence, not thinking about the answer she knew she would give, but wondering why the funny little irritating things about George didn't seem to annoy her as much as they used to. She stood up, stretching in a way she would never consider in front of a stranger: George had never been one to complain of her habit of stretching before bed.

'I'll stay, thanks very much,' she said, arms above her head. 'But no hanky-panky, mind.'

In the dim light she could tell from his amazed expression that no such thought had crossed George's mind.

'Would I ever?' he asked. 'You can trust me. But it's nice seeing you again. Just the same as ever – well, in a way. Let's go and settle you in, sheets and whatnot.'

An hour later, her case unpacked, Peggy sat up in bed wondering at the curious turn of events. Her critical eye took in the ugly maple furniture, the hideous curtains, the central light – she missed a lamp by her bed – and she felt some pity for George. To have stumbled along in such discomfort and ugliness for so long . . . but then he had never been a great observer. Probably none of this affected him in the way it would affect her.

There was a knock on the door. Peggy's hand went to her chest. One of the two nightdresses she had packed to take to Alnwick had a low-cut front. She had chosen to wear this one tonight, for no particular reason.

'Yes?'

'Everything all right?'

'Fine.'

'I'll leave a light on, on the landing.' Pause. 'If I don't see you in the morning, good luck. Drop by again.'

'Thanks.'

Well, blow me down, if he didn't come knocking on my door, Jen. The cheek of it! I told him where to get off. But the fact of the matter is, George is still attracted to me. It was as plain as anything.

Peggy slid down in the bed. Before she could dwell on what could have been, what might have been, she fell asleep, hand still protecting her unassaulted breast.

She woke next morning soon after nine – a most unusual time for her, who was usually up and hoovering at seven-thirty. Hurrying out of bed, Peggy put her lateness down to the thickness of the curtains. No chink of sun slid into the strange room. She pulled them back, annoyed with herself, and looked at a landscape of 1930s suburban villas all staring blankly over their privet hedges. Then she dressed, folded her sheets – one blue, one pink – and packed her case.

Downstairs, there was no sign of George, and no note.

He had plainly left in a hurry. Remains of his breakfast were on the kitchen table. The empty eggshell sat in a cup she had bought on the first anniversary of their marriage. They had been staying in Paignton at the time, and Peggy had been much drawn to this china donkey whose basket on his back served as an eggcup. It was painted with merry yellows and greens, imported from Spain. George, for all his immunity to pretty things, had been taken with it, too, from the start. Nowadays, of course, her taste more refined by the myriad glossy magazines she studied every month, Peggy could see herself rejecting such a donkey with some scorn. But she was touched that George should have kept it, and was still using it. Sentimental old thing, he had always been, in some ways.

Peggy made herself toast and tea, and resumed her uncomfortable position on the stool. In the morning sun the Formica roses of the table were even more dislikable than they had been the evening before, when the shandy had thankfully softened their crude edges. And the old smell of smoke was sickening. But George would never give up smoking, never. He'd die of cancer one day, as she used so often to tell him, and serve him right. Peggy did not hurry over her breakfast: she took her time looking about, memorising every detail so that, tomorrow, she would have the pleasure of describing it all to Jen.

The awfulness of the kitchen, Jen, you can't imagine . . . curtains with a vegetable motif . . .

It was all printed very clearly on her mind.

But despite her uncharitable thoughts, it would not have occurred to Peggy to leave George's house in anything but a way that would show appreciation for his hospitality. She washed up – not only their breakfast things, but the dishes from last night that were piled in the unattractive sink. She wiped down the Formica surfaces, straightened things here and there, emptied the ashtrays. Then, finding the rubbish bin full, she decided her last act of kindness would be to empty it in the dustbin outside.

I felt I should leave a good impression, if nothing else, Jen . . .

But the back door was locked. This Peggy discovered once she had struggled to undo the giant bolts screwed at top and bottom of the door. There was no key in the lock. Patiently, she began to search for it – all the obvious places, the bread bin, under tins, top of the fridge. But no luck. No key.

Next she tried the small windows over the sink. Awkwardly leaning over the draining board, she struggled with locks that were completely unfamiliar to her. So then she went to the hall. There, the bolts on the stained wood door were drawn back – but it, too, was locked. Another search for the key: this took Peggy through all the nooks and crannies of the stuffy hall, even George's coat pockets that hung dully from a row of hooks. But again no luck. Peggy sat on the stairs to think.

I was screaming mad, Jen, I can tell you. The bastard had locked me in. Imagine! I was his prisoner.

She sat quite calmly for a while, intrigued by a sort of nefarious peace that seemed to have possessed her. Then, when the hall clock stirred her with its muffled strokes of ten, she went to the table on which the old-fashioned, undusted telephone stood upon an ancient directory. Obviously George's dislike of the telephone had not changed. She looked up the number of his firm in Lincoln, amazed by the weight of the old-fashioned receiver in her hand. She was put straight through to his office. His secretary, an efficient-sounding voice, said Mr Jarrett was out seeing retailers all day and would be going home from his last appointment. No, there was no way he could be contacted. Unlike everyone else, he had always refused to have a mobile telephone. Here, the secretary allowed herself a slight giggle. Was there a message, in the unlikely event of Mr Jarrett ringing in? No, there certainly wasn't, said Peggy briskly – though she had a funny feeling her voice sounded curiously dreamy. And no, she would not be leaving her name.

The bastard, Jen. There I was, stuck. I thought, shall I ring the police?

Peggy returned to the kitchen. There, the overflowing plastic bin sat like an accusation on the threadbare linoleum of George's horrible kitchen floor. Something about it made her look round once more, and this time she saw all the things that could be done by way of improvement. A strange energy and desire to tackle them piped through her. She found an old mop, a balding broom, stiffened cloths, a packet of hardened soap powder, and set to work.

Well, I was dumbfounded. You can imagine. The cheek of it – trapped! Never occurred to me, all these years, poor old Romeo had been wanting me back . . . I just sat there, demented.

Peggy worked hard and efficiently, and it was lunchtime

by the time she had everything to her satisfaction. As good
as could be in the circumstances, considering the rotten
fabric of the place. At least the air smelt more of pine-
scented polish than of smoke . . . Pleased with herself, she
found an aged piece of cheddar in the fridge, some stale
sponge fingers and a withered apple which, had she been
less hungry, she would have thrown out. As she sat eating
in the caged silence, she thought of all the thousands of
meals George must have had here, alone, in all these years.
Did he ever cook himself something good? What had he
been thinking all those silent weekends and evenings on
his own?

Revived by the food, Peggy then went upstairs. She
crept, almost guilty, into George's bedroom. What should
have been the marital bedroom, she couldn't help thinking.
The sight was much as she imagined it would be: unmade
bed, familiar striped pyjamas and a single battered paper-
back detective novel on the floor, not a picture on the
fog-grey walls. She went at once to the windows: they, too,
were secured with the same kind of locks as downstairs.
The sour, smoky air indicated they had probably not been
opened for years. How could he bear summer nights in
such an atmosphere?

It was horrible, his room, Jen. Bleak . . .

The least she could do was tidy it up a bit, have a go at
the dust.

By the time she had finished the cleaning of George's
bedroom, and the vile bathroom – curtains of cracked plastic, plugs of old hair in bath and basin – most of the
afternoon had gone. Tired, Peggy decided to return to the

spare room for a rest. She would have to set off the moment George came home. If he did come home. For a nasty moment she was stricken with the thought that he might have some wicked plan behind her imprisonment. He might intend to leave her to sweat it out for a while: punishment for the past.

She shivered in the dead air of the spare room. Windows locked there, too. Last night she had not liked to call George in to open them. Now – tea-time it must be – the afternoon sun hot outside, it was unbearable. Better go back downstairs: cup of tea, watch television, hope the hours would not drag too much till George . . . Peggy had no energy to tackle the sitting-room, riled though she was by its dismal state. She sat on the sofa with her cup of tea, switched on a children's programme, must have dozed off.

I was mad by the time he came back, Jen. I screamed at him, I can tell you . . .

She didn't know when it was, but he was standing over her. He carried a bulging plastic carrier from a super-market, and he was smiling.

'You dropped off, then?'

'Must have.'

'Didn't expect I'd find you here.'

Peggy rallied, sleepiness quite gone. 'You locked me in, you old sod. What did you do that for?'

'I what?'

'Made me your prisoner.'

'Never. You must be daft.' He gave a small, guilty laugh.

'Every window and door in the place locked. I checked.'

'Locked, yes. That I don't deny. You know what I am

about security. But I left the key. Course I left the key.'

'Where?'

'Come with me.'

Peggy followed him into the kitchen, suddenly uncertain. George dumped the bag on the table, went to the brush mat by the door. 'Course I locked the door from the outside – necessary precaution – but I left you this.' With some triumph he lifted up a corner of the mat and picked up the key that lay on the cement floor. He waggled it in her face. 'There, Peg o' my life. What did I tell you? Where, for all those years, did we always put the key at home? Under the kitchen doormat. Thought you wouldn't have forgotten that.'

Peggy sniffed. Foolishness engulfed her. 'Well, I did. I looked everywhere.'

'Silly old you, what? Still—' He looked round in some awe. 'I see you've been doing a bit more than just looking. Tidied up a bit, haven't you? It needed a woman's hand. I'm not much good at that sort of thing, you may remember. Here.' He put his hand in his jacket pocket and pulled out a couple of packets of seeds. 'You take these. A bushy new cornflower we're trying out. You've always liked cornflowers.'

Peggy examined the packets with their optimistic illustrations.

'I haven't much of a garden,' she said.

'Mine's quite sizeable, considering,' said George.

There was silence, then Peggy thanked him and said she'd like to take them.

He tried to calm me down with a packet of his blinking free seeds, Jen: imagine. I said I don't want your seeds, George Jarrett, you can't buy me that cheaply . . .

'I'll be on my way,' she said.

'Better eat something first.' George pulled things from the bag. 'My shopping night, Wednesdays. Afraid you caught me when stocks were low, last night. We could make up for it tonight.'

Any fears Peggy had had earlier about George not taking care of himself now scattered. He had bought a selection of meats and chicken breasts and fruits and vegetables: an expensive rough pâté, French bread, and several bottles of good red wine. His tastes had changed. What was more, oddly, he seemed to have bought enough for two.

'Tell you what,' he went on, 'if you'd like to put something in the oven, I'll nip up to the greenhouse for half an hour, then I'll come back and join you in a nice glass of claret.'

. . . and then he had the cheek to ask me to cook the dinner! I said you cook your own blinking dinner. I said you haven't changed a mite, George: you and your chauvinistic ways that were the breaking of our marriage . . .

An hour later they were enjoying the pâté while the pre-made casserole warmed in the oven. George, against his better judgement, allowed Peggy to persuade him to leave the back door open so that sweet evening air pushed into the smoke and pine of the kitchen, dissipating the obnoxious smells. They drank the first bottle of wine and opened the second. By the time they were into the beautiful ripe Camembert, Peggy found herself weak with nostalgia.

'We did have some good times, George,' she allowed herself to say.

'Some, if you say so,' agreed George, and steered the conversation back to the possibility of a goldfish pond he had in mind for the bottom of the garden.

By the end of the second bottle of wine it was clear there was no possibility of Peggy driving home that night. Departure would have to be postponed once again. Still, there was no pressing reason to hurry home. So when George urged her to stay another night, she did not bother to resist. Once more he wished her a safe journey next day, and said what a nice surprise it had been, her dropping in, and he would leave the light on outside her room. Once more, despite the discomfort of the bed, Peggy fell asleep very quickly.

It was only next morning, going downstairs with my case again, Jen, I realised I'd forgotten to mention the matter of the key. I must admit fear gripped me. He'd had such a funny look in his eye the night before – nothing to do with the wine. And when I looked under the doormat, and there was no key, I knew it. I knew clearly what he was trying to do. He was trying in his horrible devious way to get me back . . . If you've ever had a man after you like that . . .

Quite calmly, Peggy boiled herself an egg for breakfast and made real coffee instead of tea. The kitchen smelt much better now: she sat looking at the lovely show of gladioli in the bed outside, hands round her mug, a comfortable summer warmth within and without. But she would not be caught out so foolishly again. When she had washed up she searched everywhere she could think of for the key to the back door. Unable to find it, she then checked the front door, and every window in the house: as yesterday, all locked. A prisoner again. She contemplated ringing George's office, but decided there would be no point: he was out on his rounds most days. And besides, she would do her best to escape this time, before he came back. This silly nonsense couldn't go on. Or could it?

The morning, Peggy thought, must at least be put to some good use. Back in the kitchen, she went through the groceries George had bought the day before and found ingredients for bread, a cake, veal stew, a gooseberry crumble. She set to work. The thought of the surprise George would have when he returned, reminding him of the good cook she had always been . . . A bee was trapped in the room. Peggy found herself sympathising with its pathetic buzzing.

'We're both prisoners, bee,' she said. 'But it's not too bad, is it?'

It was terrible, Jen, shut in, not a breath of air, dreading him with his frightening eyes coming back. What would he do tonight? Fill me with drink again? I wondered, should I ring the police? I was trembling all over by now, hardly able to think. The monster. Men who want a woman – they'll do anything.

Peggy was kneading dough with a firm hand, a slight smile on her lips. No questions as to why George had shut her in a second time came to perplex her. Rather, she found herself remembering some of the pleasures in their marriage. They had taken long walks, sometimes, in the Lake District, staying at farmhouses on the way. They both liked a bet on the horses, an occasional drink at the pub, quiet evenings in front of the television. It was hard to remember, in fact, quite what had gone so wrong. George had always been a terrible old chauvinist, never renowned for his open mind, but Peggy had become used to all that – couldn't remember the exact nature, come to think of it, of all the irritations and frustrations. Perhaps they had simply been too young, too wrapped up in their own preoccupations, no children to deflect them, to give them a mutual interest. Had they stuck it out . . . by now, they might have reached that state of coasting along in mutual tolerance that a good many people seemed to settle for. They would have had companionship, the comfort of security. Had they stuck it out . . .

I spent that afternoon Jen, going back in my mind over all the awful things about George, thinking how well rid of him I was.

She spent the afternoon impatiently waiting for the delicious things to come out of the oven (the smell of baking bread finally overcame the last traces of smoke), an idea forming in her mind. It made her restless, her idea. Too restless to weigh it up very accurately. She laid the table for tea, chivvied about, willing the hours to hurry until the evening.

'I saw your car. What happened this time?' George began, soon as he was through the door.

'It was no joke, today, George. Locked in again.'

Peggy tried to sound angry. She knew she didn't succeed.

'Don't be silly.' He stomped over to the small alarm clock on the dresser. Picked it up. Produced the key.

'I thought you said under the mat?'

'Under the mat didn't work yesterday, did it? Thought I'd

try our other place today. Remember: the key'll be under the mat or under the clock, we always said. Thought you couldn't be so . . . another day.'

'Well, I was. Stupid, I know.' George, she thought, gave her a funny look. 'There's tea in the pot.'

They both sat down at the table. George cut into the bulging loaf. The crust crackled and chipped under his eager knife.

'I say, jolly nice, this. Haven't had a bit of bread the like of this since . . .' He sniffed. 'Smells as if you've been cooking other things, too.'

'I made supper. Had to fill the hours somehow.'

'Sorry about the misunderstanding, Peg o' my life.'

'That's all right.'

There was a friendly pause. They both spread honey thickly on to the buoyant slices of bread. This is auspicious, Peggy thought. Now is my moment.

Greedy sod, got through my loaf in a flash. I could see he meant business . . .

'George,' she said, 'I could stay a few days if you like. Finish tidying the place up, put some things in the freezer for you. I mean, there's nothing pressing I have to be home for.'

'What about your little cat? I expect you've still got a cat, haven't you?'

'My neighbour Jen sees to her. I could ring Jen, tell her I was delayed for a few days.'

George sniffed again, put down his bread. His hand, his face, were suddenly, visibly, rigid. Peggy was awkward under his new look.

'Funny,' she said, 'I was thinking. You know, if we hadn't been so bloody silly we'd still be together today. None of that divorce business need have happened. We'd be quite happy, used to each other. We'd have security, company, for our old age. Not that I'm grumbling about things as they are, and you don't seem too badly off, could be a nice place here—'

'Vicious neighbourhood,' interrupted George.

'Vicious or not, we would probably have been better off together once we'd got over our ups and downs.'

In the silence that followed her little speech – not quite as she had rehearsed it to herself – George spotted the bee. Too exhausted to buzz, it now tumbled back and forth along the window ledge.

'That poor bee,' said George, at last. 'Must find the window key, let it out.'

'George, did you hear what I said?'

'I heard what you said, Peggy.'

'And what do you think?'

'I think, not on your life, Peg o' my heart. Not for anything. Too much damage caused, no one changed that much, probably. I'm used to it here, as I am. Happy, like.'

There was a silence. Peggy longed for the bee to resume its buzzing. But it had given up.

'Very well. It was just a suggestion.'

'You were always superior to me, see. I didn't like that.'

'Nothing's ever perfect.'

George looked round his newly cleaned kitchen.

'Thank you for tidying up, though. I'll try to keep it . . . You finish your tea. I must get down to the watering.'

George stood up, impatient to be off. Peggy had no appetite for the rest of her bread and honey.

'Keep in touch,' she said.

'Why not? Card at Christmas. That sort of thing. Drive carefully.' He pecked her on the cheek.

'I will.'

Peggy turned her head so that he should not see her face. Ten minutes later she was on her way, suitcase and bunch of hastily picked farewell marigolds on the seat beside her.

She was eager to be home now, could not wait to tell Jen. She arrived before midnight, so rang at once. Jen was a night bird, would be longing to hear from her. She had probably been worrying about why she had not returned on the promised day.

'Jen, it's me, Peggy. Just back. *What* a time, I can tell you. I've been with George. Yes, George, ex-husband George. Trapped! Almost raped! Begged me to stay, wanted me back, *locked me in* for two days till I managed to escape. *I was his prisoner*, Jen! Honestly!'

Peggy kept her friend up for a long time with her story.

Squirrels

Vera Brindle lived alone in a state of dishevelled solitude which the social workers who called upon her could not believe was desirable. They had begun their interfering ways some years ago now and their visits to her cottage were becoming more frequent. One or other of them – sometimes two together like policemen on the beat in a dangerous area – would knock on the door and, when there was no answer, press their faces to the downstairs windows, sheltering their eyes with both hands. Vera Brindle would watch the intruders from upstairs, hidden behind a curtain. On the rare occasions she gave in and opened the door, they would put to her the suggestion of a 'little chat over a cup of tea'. Vera, who disliked both tea and chats, would wave them into the kitchen and enjoy watching their incredulous faces as they looked around the room, making their assessments. She would make no move to put on the kettle. As for the 'chat' they were hoping for – that, too, they quickly discovered, was to be denied them.

Only last week a new young girl had been sent to try out her persuasive powers to make Vera Brindle 'see sense', as they put it. This particular representative of those who know best wore an anxious-about-deprived-people expression which, the old lady knew very well, would be switched off when she went home at five-thirty. She could just imagine the girl hurrying to the kind of party where the boasts of the caring professions meant instant admiration. The girl's narrow little face was contorted with the sort of professional sympathy that made Vera Brindle determine to be unhelpful.

'You must be Ms Vera Brindle,' said this unwelcome creature, when the door was opened a few inches. She was dressed in ugly clothes that signalled there was no frivolity in her do-gooding soul, and hideous, earnest shoes of yellowish leather.

'No, I'm Miss Brindle. I've been Miss Brindle all my life, so there's no supposing, my young girl, I'm going to change to some fashionable title now. And who may you be?'

'I'm Lee Barker. Social Services. But do call me Lee.'

'Certainly shan't do any such thing. I don't know you.' Vera Brindle edged the door open a little wider. She noted the intruder's bony nostrils rear up as various smells began their assault. 'I shall call you Miss Barker, unless you tell me you are a Mrs.' She sniffed. 'Which I very much doubt. Come in, Miss Barker.'

'I don't want us to get off on the wrong foot,' Lee Barker said, once they were in the kitchen. 'I wouldn't want that at all.' Her eyes carried on scouring every crevice of the kitchen. Perhaps she had been warned there was no use asking for a cup of tea, for they did not pause on the kettle. Vera Brindle, enjoying the young woman's unease, kept her silence. She listened to the scrabblings of the squirrels in the roof. Drat the squirrels, she thought. They were usually quiet at this time of day. If this cheeky young do-gooder heard them she'd start writing all sorts of exaggerated reports in her notebook, threaten to send along the pest control man.

'I have news for you, Vera,' Lee Barker said at last. 'There's a nice council flat come up, just a mile or so from Exeter. One of those sheltered housing arrangements. A lovely warden, should you need anything. All mod cons.'

Vera Brindle snorted, furious at the persistent attempt at intimacy, and enraged by the suggestion. But it was useless, she knew, trying to explain that mod cons held no allure. While she could scornfully understand they were part of contemporary utopia, they did not feature on her own list of essentials to a happy life.

'I'm not Vera to you,' she said.

'Sorry. *Miss* Brindle.' Lee Barker gave a patronising smile, which exposed a flash of brown teeth edging a long expanse of gum. Her breath smelt vile. 'Now, have you taken in what I'm saying?'

'I have and I'm not interested. I don't know why you bother yourselves, waste your time, keep coming here. Give the flat to someone who needs it. I'm all right. I'm not moving.'

Vera Brindle put a hand on the table to steady herself. She was not used to speaking at such length. So many words dizzied her. She felt exhausted, but knew she must gather her strength to tell this young woman to go.

'So you can be off now,' she said. The squirrels were scrabbling harder.

'*Miss* Brindle,' Lee Barker sneered, 'there's no use pussy-footing around any more. My colleagues and I have done our best to make you see sense. The time has come for plain speaking. This—' she looked up at the dark ceiling—'your home, is generally considered unfit for human habitation. We fear for your own safety, Miss Brindle, if you choose to stay. Why, you're not even on the telephone. What if—?'

Miss Brindle licked her lips with the point of a small green tongue. They tasted of salt. Beneath the tight caul of their skin she could feel a prickling, a singing, in their blood. She knew that if she uttered another word her mouth would explode. Teeth, lips, tongue still attached to the messy glob of its roots, would blast off from her face and splatter across the room. So she said nothing, nodded towards the door.

Lee Barker, whose anger prowled up and down her face in mauve coils, responded to the utter negativeness of the stubborn old cow, as this Brindle witch was known in the office, by pushing her nose into a handkerchief. The offensive implications of this gesture Vera Brindle chose to ignore.

'Very well, I shall go for now. But be warned.' Lee Barker's eyes, even in the poor light, were bright with indignation.

'You'd better be warned, too.' Vera Brindle was determined to have the last word, though unsure of her exact meaning.

Lee Barker swung out, tossed her nasty little trousered hips from side to side as she hurried down the path, trailing her hand along the top of the dead lavender bushes. Vera Brindle waited until she was out of sight, then sat down at the kitchen table. She pulled towards her the white plastic weighing-machine that stood like a single symbol of modernity among the debris all around it. A little weighing, she thought, would calm her down. She reached for a slab of very old cake, broke off the hard end, placed it on the plastic dish. One and a half ounces, the clock said. Vera Brindle loved that moment, when the thin red hand raced so confidently to the exact weight. She added a few crumbs. The hand wavered. Miss Brindle smiled. The weighing-machine was the best toy she had ever had. It kept her occupied for much of the day. The interest of guessing what things might weigh, only to discover how right or wrong she was, almost obsessed her. The fluctuating of weight, as bits were added or taken away to the tray, gave her a strange thrill – the same kind of thrill as sudden icicles on a winter morning, or the drone of bees busy among the apple-blossom. Finished with the cake, Miss Brindle took a handful of nuts from the bag of squirrel food. Two ounces, she reckoned. Perhaps just over. She was happy again. Lee Barker and her threats had vanished from her mind.

Vera Brindle had lived in her cottage, a mile from a small village on Exmoor, all her life. Her father had been head gamekeeper on the Bancrofts' estate. Her mother, a house-maid in the big house, had died when Vera was twelve. All she had left was a very large and cumbersome old bicycle, which Vera still rode into the village once a week to collect her provisions. (She could get an astonishing amount into the copious wicker basket that rested, squeaking, on the front mudguard.) Not long after Mrs Brindle's death, her husband's employer had sold the estate and moved abroad. The sale did not include the cottage. With his usual generosity to those who worked for him, Lord Bancroft gave the cottage – only worth a few hundred pounds – to Sam Brindle, in recognition of many years of service. This noble gesture gave a new life to Miss Brindle's father, who for some time had been cast in the immovable gloom of a widower. Now a proud house-owner himself, he set about repairs and with a friend rethatched the roof. This was the happiest time Miss Brindle could remember. Once she had left the village school, she stayed at home, with no urge to explore a wider world, looking after her father and the cottage. In those days, there was fresh paint, new carpet, uncracked windows and an up-to-date calendar on the wall each year.

But this idyllic period did not last for long. Her father, too rigorously stoking the boiler, suffered a heart attack and died two days before his daughter's twenty-first birthday. She broke up the iced cake she and her father were to have shared, and put it out for the birds. It was then she first began to take note of the squirrels, whose grabbing of the food was so much more sly than the birds'. It was then she took up a pencil and paper for the first time since she had left school, and began to make quick sketches. The results, she was in no doubt, were quite pleasing, if not perfect. She began to pin these drawings on the walls. She became aware of a faint sense of achievement.

Once her father was buried, Miss Brindle made some effort to take part in village life. There were those who feared for her loneliness, lack of company – her safety, even. She tried hard to convince them she enjoyed her solitary life and politely turned down most invitations. After a harvest supper, in her twenty-fifth year, a local farmer proposed marriage behind the barn. But Miss Brindle saw this was inspired by nothing more than quantities of beer and the hope of a more instant accomplishment than marriage itself. She took the precaution of not only turning him down, but of giving him so little hope that he thought it not worth the journey to her cottage when he sobered up.

For some years – her squirrel drawings acting as a qualification – Miss Brindle taught painting in the village school. She gave this up during the War to help out in the local hospital. Surrounded by so much death, she became alarmed by the shortness of life. Except for her weekly shopping expedition and an occasional bus journey to the dentist, she spent the best part of the next fifty years in the cottage or its small garden, feeding and drawing the squirrels, birdsong her only music when the old wireless finally broke down in 1951. Always a good needlewoman, she earned just enough money by taking in alterations and mending. To the amazement of those left in the almost deserted village, Vera Brindle seemed happy to lead this uneventful existence. She was never ill, never wanted for anything. A weird old bird, she became; a witchy threat to children. 'Vera Brindle will get you,' mothers would say. 'Vera Brindle lives with the squirrels and casts her spells.'

On the evening of Lee Barker's visit, such an agreeable plan came to Vera Brindle's mind that the social worker's unpleasant behaviour was almost forgotten. She would order a bigger weighing-machine. Fond though she was of the present one, Miss Brindle knew there was a limit to what it could accommodate. And by now she was well acquainted with the weight of most things around her: a slice of cheese, a single slipper, a bag of nuts, two pencils and a rubber. It would be exciting to try out some larger objects, things that would not cause the red hand to dash right out of sight where it hid, alarmed by so much weight, in the bowels of the machine. It would be exciting to weigh the kettle – with and without water – her boots, her big wooden paint-box. With such plans in mind, Miss Brindle began to look forward to the postman's next visit, when he would bring the new mail order catalogue in which weighing-machines of all shapes and sizes were advertised. She would send off for one at once. Fill in the form with capital letters; by then she would surely have found her old biro. She would pay by postal order. Then wait impatiently for the parcel – new things to be weighed all lined up and waiting. Already she could see herself unpacking the machine, making a space for it on the table. The sweetness of anticipation began to seep through her. She had learnt, in her solitude, that the occasional arranging of treats for yourself is the way to divide up time, cause a ripple in the otherwise smooth surface. She had discovered that antici-pation of small pleasures, to those who live alone, is a necessity. A rhythm must be created in which there are times of exceptional happiness to counteract the occasions of amorphous melancholy.

So engrossed was Vera Brindle in the thought of her new machine, that at first she did not hear the thunder. She thought the rumbling was the squirrels again. They always danced more loudly at night.

But when, soon after nine, she went to draw the pitiful curtain across the kitchen window, she felt a stab of cold wind pressing through the space between long-dead putty and old glass. As she grabbed the material in her hand, lightning turned the small panes to the colour of watered milk, and she could see they were splattered with hard rain. Vera Brindle shivered, and longed for bed. On her way upstairs, she realised that more crashing above her was indeed thunder. Feeling the bones of the wooden stairs creak beneath her, she clung to the oak rail until the trumpeting outside had stopped. Storms held no fear for her. She had faith in the protection of the cottage, though in the hurricane of 1987 she remembered the cottage walls trembled as trees in the nearby woods fell to the ground with high-pitched, splintered screams.

Vera Brindle turned on the dim light by her bed. She saw that a piece of ceiling had fallen on to the floor. She kicked at the mound of crumbled plaster, automatically wondering what it might weigh. She decided not to sweep it up till morning and glanced up at the black hole it had left. The ceiling all around it was as cracked as an old cup. If the social workers had seen it, they would have gone potty. But it didn't worry Vera Brindle. She was used to it. For so many years, lying in bed, trying to sleep, her eyes would journey over the familiar pathways of lines, the patches that bulged, the baubles of paintwork that reminded her of withered balloons at the end of a children's Christmas party in the Church Hall . . . Long ago, it had occurred to her to have the room re-plastered. But then the thought of the invasion – builders, ladders, wireless, tea – was too awful to contemplate, and the moment passed. As time went by and the ceiling deteriorated, but never collapsed, Vera Brindle's faith in it continued. It would see her out, she thought. Once she was dead, if the whole place crashed to the ground, so long as the squirrels were not hurt, she did not care.

For a moment, unnerved by the whiteness of the plaster on her bruised and threadbare carpet, Miss Brindle considered moving to her parents' room. But no, that was inconceivable. No one had ever slept in there since they died. Their high brass bed was still tightly made up with clean cotton sheets. The piece of carbolic soap, still in the dish on the wash-stand, had been used by old Mrs Barley when she came to lay out Sam Brindle. His daughter could not bear to disturb the room. Besides, her own was quite safe. What on earth had come over her, such a thought?

Avoiding the spread of white dust, she took off her skirt but kept on the rest of her clothes against the cold night. The thunder seemed to be lumbering off elsewhere; just the odd rumble now. But the squirrels were disturbed. They charged back and forth, scrambled about in the darkness of the roof, a mysterious place which Vera Brindle could never quite imagine. Their scurrying footsteps brought to mind different things: most vigorously, the noise of waves on a grey shale beach she had once visited with her mother. That was the day Mrs Brindle had given up her own long wool scarf to her daughter, as they stood pondering the winter sea, saying 'You take it, child – your weak chest.

Never do to catch a chill.' While all the time, as Miss Brindle later learned, it was her mother who had the weak chest, who was to die of pneumonia. So often, in the subterranean part of her soul, she had wondered . . . if only she had not taken the scarf, her mother might not have died. Just as clearly, the squirrels revived another sound: the kidney-shaped beans made of glass. They were kept in a jar on the high shelf above the kitchen range, only brought down as a treat on Sunday. Vera would be allowed to tip them out of the jar on to the scrubbed table. They would tumble out with a rush, fast as a small shoal of sparkling fish they came, crimson and sapphire and emerald, sparkling with lights. She would cup her hands around the mound they made, terrified lest one should escape and fall to the floor. Mrs Brindle would carefully choose a few of the beans to make flower patterns. Such imaginative leaves, she made with the green ones. 'How do you do it, Ma?' the child Vera would cry. Her own attempts at flowers were nothing like as good. 'Easy,' Mrs Brindle would say, and shuffle her bent white fingers through the pile of glass, pouncing on exactly the right one needed for her next petal. Vera, despairing at her own lack of talent in this favourite game, would simply run the beans through her fingers, loving the tinkle they made on her palm that was quite different from the scurrying noise they made as they jostled on to the table . . . That jar of glass beans, where was it now? Vera Brindle had never thrown it out. Perhaps it was still at the back of a cupboard somewhere. Might be worth looking for. She would like to weigh the beans, should she find them, on her new machine . . .

Some time much later in the night – no streak of moon-light or dawn paling the curtainless window – Vera Brindle was woken by a thump on her bed. She switched on the light. Edward, the shyest of all the squirrels, was poised, terrified, on the blankets over her feet, claws dug deep into the wool stuff. He stared ahead, not looking at her, jowls twitching almost too fast to see, tail raised high, ready to bolt.

Miss Brindle did not move, but looked up at the ceiling to see the hole was bigger; there was more powdered plaster on the carpet. Poor Edward, what a trauma, falling through the ceiling, she thought. On the other hand, she could not resist a feeling of great pleasure. For so long she had been trying to tame Edward, but he had always eluded her. His father Ernest, a huge animal with reddish eye-brows, spent more time in the kitchen than he did outdoors, while his wife, the lovely but greedy Rose, was a menace among the shelves. Edward's many brothers and sisters, cousins, uncles and aunts had all established that Vera Brindle's cottage was a perfect refuge, both as a place of hibernation and a source of food. They all had their names: the year each one was born was clear in Miss Brindle's memory. And, despite her failing sight, she could identify which junior members of the clan swung and squealed high in the trees. They were her family. She knew and loved them all. In return for her hospitality, they would keep her company just when she most needed it, perching on her chair, or shoulder, or sometimes on her head.

But Edward, strangely ungregarious, could never be won over. This was one of the great puzzles in Vera Brindle's life.

Sometimes she mentioned it when she went to the Post Office to collect her pension, but the busy woman behind the counter, with her orange lipstick, didn't seem interested. And when she tried to tell Jack the poacher, who occasionally passed by, all he had to say was that she was a stupid old woman who should clear the vermin out of her house or the authorities would be after her. He was sensitive to the authorities, was Jack, skulking about after dark. But Vera Brindle held them in no respect. If she wanted to entertain squirrels in her house, she had every right to do so, and no one could force her to evict them.

Up until this extraordinary moment in the middle of the night, Vera Brindle had never managed to persuade Edward indoors, no matter how many saucers of bread and milk, or nuts, she tempted him with, or what olden-days songs she quietly sang – a device which always intrigued the female squirrels. The unexpectedness of his arrival caused her head to spin for a moment. What should she do to reassure him? Her instinct was to put out a hand, coo a few words, offer him a biscuit from her bedside table. But no, she thought, she must resist. Lie down with as little movement as possible, put out the light, pray to the good Lord young Edward would feel at ease at last.

In the dark, she felt a small movement over her feet. Sleepy, she imagined Edward might be sleepy, too. But in the morning he was gone. When Vera Brindle let his large gang of relations in for breakfast, he was not among them.

Later that day, she stood on a chair in her bedroom and filled the hole in her ceiling with a wadding of old rags and dishcloths. She decided not to secure it further with sticking plaster, in the small hope that Edward might fall on to her bed again. His rejection had caused a smarting in her heart that was hard to dismiss, despite the sunny day. The feeling was mixed with pity for his shocking experience, and her own pleasure at having at last come so close to him.

Vera Brindle ordered her new weighing-machine from the next catalogue and waited for its arrival with a force of impatience that made her restless. She found herself unable to concentrate on anything for very long. No sooner had she sat down in her chair to peel a potato than she darted up to look out of the window. An official-looking brown envelope was delivered one day. She took it to the door, spent a long time trying to light a match with trembling fingers, and at last set light to it. It was with considerable glee that she watched the unread threats devoured by a sudden curl of flame. They were followed by a wisp of black smoke that ventured out into the rain and was instantly extinguished. Pleased though she was by her act of conflagration, a fine wire of anxiety now threaded through the impatience; they would be after her again with their suggestions. Vera Brindle turned back so sharply into the kitchen that she alarmed the squirrels feeding from their breakfast bowl of nuts. They scampered away with unusual speed.

That October, there seemed to be interminable rain. The day the postman Alfred came with the parcel, it poured down so hard that the end of the garden was no more than a smudged outline. The guardian trees beyond were scarcely visible against the grey sky. Alfred's waterproof cape, as he hurried up the path, produced no more than a low-watt shine, a flash of dulled yellow. He stood at the door, holding out the parcel, dripping. Much though Vera Brindle dreaded anyone in her kitchen, she felt obliged to ask him in. The poor man was wet through.

Alfred stepped through the door. Vera Brindle quickly relieved him of the parcel, laid it in the space she had cleared days ago in readiness for its arrival. Once he had gone, this huge, wet, friendly man, she would unwrap it infinitely slowly, rolling up the string, folding the paper . . . Alfred's cape dripped on the floor. Raindrops glinted on his white moustache.

'Sorry,' he said.

'That's no matter. Would you fancy a cup of warm milk?'

Alfred, who had been hoping for the more conventional offer of tea, arranged his face into an appreciative smile of acceptance. He stood awkwardly by the sink, his cap just brushing the drooping ceiling. This was the first time in twenty-four years the Brindle witch had asked him in. He had delivered post to her in far worse weather than this. What, he wondered, did the invitation mean? Would she offer him a nut as well as the milk? There seemed to be bowls of nuts everywhere . . . as if ready for a drinkless party. Something to tell the wife, this.

The postman began to look around. In the rain-dark room, nothing was very clear. But he could make out that the walls were completely covered with old scraps of paper, all browned to some degree with age, they were, and uniformly stuck to the wall with a black drawing pin at the left-hand corner, the rest of the paper left free. Altogether, they gave a shaggy impression, a feeling that the walls were ruffled up to keep out the cold, like a bird's breast. Very peculiar, very rum. But Alfred could see that the position-ing of the scraps of paper was something of a work of art in itself. They were methodically placed, just overlapping, like a tiled roof. Very precise, very clever.

Vera Brindle handed Alfred a cup of tepid milk. He moved to peer closer at the strange wallcovering. Each one was a sketch, he could just see, sometimes a painting, of a squirrel – sometimes just part of a squirrel, a faded leg, a tail at many angles. The pictures were faded almost to extinc-tion, only beady eyes, with minute highlights, remained distinct. For all that, Alfred – a man, he liked to think, of some artistic appreciation – could see the drawing was fine, sensitive. The Brindle witch was a talented old bird.

'These are beautiful,' he said. 'Bloody marvellous. You could make a fortune, selling squirrel pictures.'

Vera Brindle, who was anxious for Alfred to drink his milk quickly and go, shrugged. The time for appreciation of her art was long past. She was not interested in anything to do with fortunes.

'I don't do it any more,' she said. 'Paints all dried up.'

'Pity, that.'

They stood without talking while Alfred gulped the sour, tepid milk. Rain clattered more heavily against the windows.

'Mustn't keep you from your rounds,' said Vera Brindle at last.

'No.' Alfred brushed milk and rain from his moustache with the back of his hand. His huge presence in the kitchen had turned it into a strange, unrecognisable place that unnerved Miss Brindle. She wished he would hurry.

Alfred stepped out into the rain. He was glad to regain air that smelt of sodden grass and leaves. The stench in the kitchen – rotten food, mould, wet animals? he could not quite place it – had been almost overpowering. He turned to bid Vera Brindle goodbye. She was beside him, rain darkening her clothes.

'You go back in. You'll get a soaking.'

'I'll come to the end with you.'

'I shouldn't advise that, Miss Brindle. Look, you're soaked already.'

But she was walking up the path to the gate with determined stride.

'As for your roof—' The postman spoke more loudly. She was a yard ahead of him now, astonishingly fast on her slippered feet. He wanted her to hear. 'I was thinking, coming in, you should get that seen to. Looks dangerous to me.'

Vera Brindle reached the gate before turning to face him, face shining as rain squiggled down the furrowed skin, sparse white hair sticking up in small points. Her eyes moved scornfully to the roof of the cottage. There was, indeed, a grave dip in the thatch – she had not looked at it for some years. But quickly she realised Alfred was as foolish as the social workers; the roof had been expertly thatched by her own father not sixty years ago and had never caused a moment's trouble, apart from the odd starling caught up in the wire.

'Look at that moss,' she snapped. 'That's been there for years. That protects the thatch, moss.'

'That moss,' began Alfred. But he could see the pointlessness of arguing in the rain.

'I'm not worried,' said Vera Brindle. She gave him a brief wave and was hurrying up the path before he had time to thank her for the milk.

So engrossed in her new weighing-machine was Vera Brindle that she did not notice the persistence of the rain, or its heaviness. She delighted in the hours as she weighed all manner of new things – writing her guessed weight, followed by their actual weight, with her old biro. By evening, she became aware of a smell of damp that was perhaps stronger than usual, though it was always like that on a rainy day. It meant the squirrels would want to come in earlier. She opened the window for them – a pool of rainwater on the sill flopped on to the floor – long before it was dark.

On her way to bed that night, carrying the weighing-machine under her arm, Vera Brindle felt an almost tangible sense of well-being. It could rain every day till Christmas, for all she cared; she would spend her time weighing so many things on both machines. (It was important, she thought, not to desert the old one, just because of the newcomer. Mustn't hurt its feelings.)

In her room there was a pile of rags and dishcloths on the floor. They were mixed with more crumbled plaster. The hole in the ceiling was much bigger – funny she hadn't heard it fall. And at the end of the bed sat Edward, reddish elbows just twitching, watching her.

Vera Brindle managed to stand quite still, wondering what to do. She put her free hand into the pocket of her cardigan, found a couple of nuts, considered throwing these towards Edward. But she quickly abandoned that idea. Nothing must be done to alarm him. So she placed the nuts in the tray of the weighing-machine and put it gently on the floor. Still Edward did not move. His eye was bright as all squirrels' eyes; Vera Brindle suddenly remembered the tiny sable brush which she used for the white highlights in her paintings. After a while, she pulled back the blankets on her bed, slipped into it, not bothering even to remove her slippers. The most important thing in the world, having come this far, was not to scare away Edward now. In bed, awkwardly perched against the pillows, Vera Brindle studied his small body, tense as a trap, ready to pounce at the slightest sign of danger. Rain beat in angry swarms against the small windows. It was cold.

For some time, Vera Brindle lay unmoving, waiting. Then Edward suddenly jumped off the bed, with lashing tail, to the top of the pile of rags and leapt into the plastic tray of the weighing-machine. The noise of his nails, scratching the plastic, unnerved him. But in a moment he was calm enough to attend to the nuts. He clasped one of them in his paws, his jaws working with frantic speed. Vera Brindle, still very cold but dizzy with excitement, strained to see what the machine clock registered. But without her glasses it was impossible. She made a silent guess.

Then she allowed herself a contented sigh. The extraordinary sight, not a yard from her, was beyond her most unlikely dreams. The weighing of a squirrel . . . her ultimate, most secret desire. No one would ever believe her claim that the squirrel had taken it upon himself to jump on to the machine. But that was of no importance, as there was no one to tell. The shock of it all wearied her more than she could have supposed. Her clothes were still damp from the rain. She shivered. Up in the roof above her, Edward's relations began their nightly dance, their tapping feet almost in time with the rain. Very peculiar, she thought, as she fell asleep.

Vera Brindle dreamed of dozens of squirrels lining up to be weighed and of Edward, quite tame now, visiting her every day. She dreamed of sun on her mother's opal ring and the noise of waves breaking on the grey shale. Their crashing became so loud they briefly woke her. For a moment she saw that moonlight on the windows, shredded by rain, lit a room in turmoil: chunks of rock – was it? – on the floor. Black spaces in the ceiling. She heard more crashing, thudding, the high screams of terrified squirrels. Then she saw them raining down on her, flashes of tooth, eye, frantic tail. How kind they were, coming to comfort her. Behind them, she could see a huge slab of ceiling, shifting, unhurried as a cloud. She shut her eyes and struggled to breathe beneath a sudden new weight. Never in all her years of weighing, she thought, would she have imagined her family of squirrels to be so heavy.

Some days later, Alfred the postman returned to Vera Brindle's cottage with another brown envelope. It still rained, and he saw that the thatched roof had fallen in, breaking up the livid green covering of moss.

The kitchen door was locked, the windows shut. Alfred called loudly, but there was no reply. He peered through the kitchen window and could see that among the chaos of things on the table a squirrel lay on its side. He could not tell if it was alive or dead. An iciness went through him, nothing to do with the weather. He hurried away, reported what he had seen.

The rain had at last begun to ease a little when Lee Barker and her colleague, both in turbid anoraks, drove to the cottage. They had brought with them a small metal ladder on the roof-rack. They carried it between them down the muddy path, elated by their feeling of smugness. This would teach the old girl not to listen to those who knew best.

'Stupid daft witch,' said Lee Barker, in her off-duty voice. 'This'll make her see sense at last. The sooner she's sitting round the telly in an old people's home, the better for all of us. We can't keep putting up with all this aggravation.'

'Quite,' said her colleague.

Like Alfred, they received no response from knocking on the downstairs windows. With a gesture of some triumph, therefore, Lee Barker stuck her ladder into what had once been a flower bed beneath Vera Brindle's window. Clumsily she climbed, her huge trainers hesitant on the metal rungs of the ladder.

'Got the mobile on you, Di? Expect we'll need an ambulance.'

'Operation Witch Evacuation, right.' Di, awkward on the spongy grass, tapped her mobile telephone and laughed. She watched her friend push away lumps of rotten thatch that hung over the casement window and look in, pressing her face to the small panes.

Lee Barker screwed up her professional eyes and saw

that there was life in the bedroom. There were squirrels everywhere. They ran up and down over huge lumps of plaster on the bed, where Vera Brindle lay facing the window. She stared back with dull but open eyes. Sitting on the old woman's hand was a squirrel with reddish elbows, a small tuft of her white hair between its paws.

*M*istral

I don't know why, and there is nothing I can do about it, but I have this way of irritating people. It's a sad affliction but, as I am unable to change matters, every day is a minefield. I know that at any moment I am liable to do or say something that causes Mr Arthur or Mr Gerald such annoyance they can barely trust themselves to speak.

My name is Annie Hawker. I am housekeeper to Mr Arthur and Mr Gerald, and have held that position for eleven years. Both gentlemen are in their mid-sixties. Mr Arthur was once briefly married to a certain Lucretia. The very thought of this lady brings out the worst in him, though her name is rarely mentioned. There are two grown-up children: Deirdre and Brian. Both of them are over thirty, unmarried, and still searching their way in life. Their telephone calls to their father don't inspire much sympathy. I hear him snarling down the telephone several times a week, though I have reason to believe he is a generous father, and sends cheques to England with some frequency. When Deirdre and Brian come for a visit – some would call it a prolonged free holiday, as I'm bound to observe to Mr Arthur – tension in the house rises. Mr Arthur gets no pleasure from their company, and the feeling is all too plainly mutual. Well, I have to say it: they aren't very rewarding offspring: lumpen, dull minds, lazy, spoiled, purposeless.

Their visits put Mr Gerald into a bad temper, too. He stomps off most mornings, walks the hills or visits friends all day, and then is barely civil to them over dinner. Jealous, I suppose. Mr Gerald was never married, and the children remind him of Mr Arthur's past. Or it may be that he simply finds their ungrateful presence in the house annoying. Which it is. Secretly, all three of us look forward to their departure.

I took the job two years after my husband Simon died in an industrial accident. Arm torn off in a machine in the mill, and he wasn't even a manual worker, but an inspector. Trouble was, he was always poking his nose – in this case, his arm – too far into things, being a conscientious inspector. I knew in my bones some disaster would happen one day. So I wasn't surprised by the amputation, or the complications that followed. Or indeed his death within the week. Nor did I waste much time grieving his departure. Our marriage had never been of a high calibre: we had just chuntered along for ten years, childless, him travelling round the North inspecting, me working for the Inland Revenue.

I had always had a secret inclination to write. But I knew there was no hope there, for all that I was good at essays at school. Everyone wants to write and thinks they can. But there was no evidence to make me believe I'd be any good, or stand a chance of publication. So I abandoned that dream in order to avoid disappointment, and funnily enough quite enjoyed my time at the Inland Revenue.

Anyhow, two years after Simon's death the thought came to me: now's your chance, Annie, I thought. Make a dash for it before you're too old. Go for a complete change. Try a new life.

I started looking at advertisements for jobs abroad, and as luck would have it came upon Mr Arthur and Mr Gerald's within days. The description of the place appealed to me – hilltop cluster of houses in the Luberon region of France. Beautiful scenery, peace, swimming pool, sun: the stuff of most people's dreams.

They were interviewing applicants for the job in London. I went down the night before, stayed with my sister in Barnet so as not to be in a fuss on the morning. I dressed carefully in a nice navy suit and pink blouse. It occurred to me a younger type of person would probably be applying for the job, of the jeans and tee-shirt school, the kind who care more about being in the sun than what they give in return. I wanted to make a good impression, assure them of my reliability, willingness to work hard, and above all my unfailing sense of humour.

Well, it worked. They were a little stiff, the two gentlemen, sitting side by side on a plumped-up sofa. Very tanned, they were, with almost identical thin grey hair. In a word, we liked each other from the start. 'Do call me Annie,' I said, when the interview was concluded. 'None of this Mrs Hawker stuff, now, if you please.' They smiled a little instead of agreeing to this, and made no reciprocal proposal. I realised at once that they were the sort of gentlemen who, at their age, liked to retain a little of the old-school formality, and hoped I had not blundered in my friendly suggestion. Evidently I had not, for they offered me the job, two days later.

Just a week later I fell in love with Le Beau Banc at first sight. They had bought the place, a deserted hillside hamlet, some twenty years before, built a road (still pretty rocky) and renovated the whole place with great skill and imagination. Today, the small houses are a monument to local craftsmen: beautifully converted with mellow tiled floors and lime-washed walls, their old shutters scrubbed and oiled, their old beams stripped and sealed. One of these – quite the nicest, I think, with its little terrace overlooking a vast valley that is always blue with either lavender or mist, is entirely mine. A very far cry from our house in Sheffield, I can tell you. I put up my few things – my picture of Morecambe Bay and my mother's shell mirror and so on – and it felt like home from the start. I can't imagine living anywhere else.

Mr Gerald, being a keen and skilled gardener, planted the whole place, too. There are peach and olive trees, English roses and mimosa. Every path is lined with lavender, and a huge fig tree shades their terrace. Butterflies flutter all day and the crickets sing every evening, ruffling the silence. Oh, it's paradise, as I tell my sister. I know how lucky I am.

The original idea, Mr Arthur told me, was to make the place a kind of commune or colony for artists and writers. The plan was that each would have their individual house in which they worked in peace, and meet for dinner in the evening. But long before my arrival this plan failed. It seemed many a young so-called artist, plus boy- or girlfriend, checked in for a long free holiday full of delights of a certain kind, but in which little artistically was accomplished. So they decided only to put friends and relations in the guest houses: they themselves live in the large main house, which is my responsibility.

To be honest, in all these years I have never quite discovered what Mr Arthur and Mr Gerald actually do. Obviously they are gentlemen of some means, and have no need of regular employment. But Mr Gerald seems always to be on one of the many telephones in his study, often to auction houses in London and New York, as far as I can gather. Very thick expensive art magazines arrive for him every week, and sometimes foreign gentlemen come for lunch. On those occasions Mr Gerald suggests I cook something French rather than the Yorkshire favourites we have on our own. The guests bring with them such funny-looking old ceramic pots which they handle with great care, and talk about in low voices.

Mr Arthur, in his study, is on the telephone a great deal of the time, too, and I understand he has interests in South Africa. But it doesn't bother me that I don't know the exact nature of their professions. All that concerns me is what I have to do to be satisfactory in my job: and that I know precisely.

My employers are gentlemen of routine. They thrive on the domestic timetables they have devised for themselves, and I do my best to see they are not interrupted. It's not hard to take care of them in the manner which they enjoy, because they are easy to please as long as everything is spick and span and meals are on time. They pay me a very fair wage and give me plenty of money for housekeeping, so I am able to call in a plumber or electrician, if need be, and pay him, without having to bother one of the gentlemen.

My day starts early. I'm in the kitchen by seven, all nice and orderly as I've left it the night before. I step outside, enjoying the early morning before the sun has become too hot, and pick a ripe peach or fig for the bowl. I lay the table, blue and terracotta cups and plates from a local pottery, put croissants in the oven and the coffee in the jug. Mr Arthur and Mr Gerald appear regular as clockwork at eight o'clock, each in his blue-and-white kimono.

'Morning, Mr Gerald Mr Arthur,' I say. 'Had a good night, have we?'

I have to admit they don't answer me any more because, I believe, although they appreciate my question is the height of good manners, they don't want to bother me with the troubles of their nights. (Mr Arthur suffers from asthma, Mr Gerald has problems with his digestion.) But I always like to be polite and show an interest. It used to worry me when they gave up answering, but I don't mind any more. I'm used to their ways and they're used to mine.

To be quite honest, the position of housekeeper is an amorphous one, not easy. The problem of address, for a start. I appreciated they wanted to maintain their little bar-rier, to denote my position as employee rather than friend. So when they insisted on calling me Mrs Hawker I did not object, and soon got used to it. They did make one big concession: I should not call them *sir*, they said, this being a newly democratic world, and as they both had compli-cated double-barrelled names Mr Arthur and Mr Gerald was the compromise we settled on. That was how they had been addressed by the staff at home as children, they explained, and thought it a charming custom. I agreed.

To begin with, I found it hard to know what was expected of me. What exactly was my place? I never asked the question specifically and they never made it clear to me. Normally, for instance, I would lunch with them at the kitchen table, or on the terrace, but the invitation was never extended should there be a visitor, no matter how often that person came. For some reason they always liked to dine on their own, so once their food is cooked and on the table I have to hang around waiting to clear away. I mean, I've never got on with watching French television – after all these years I haven't managed to grasp the French language at all, though I'm pretty good at making myself understood in the shops. So the evenings are a little bleak, though I enjoy my knitting, or my latest Catherine Cookson. Then again, it's a little confusing when people come for a drink. 'Fetch the bottle of Chablis out of the fridge, if you will, Mrs Hawker,' says Mr Arthur, and in a moment I'm placing it on the table by the sofa, on a tray with six crystal glasses and a pottery bowl of fresh olives. 'And have one yourself, Mrs Hawker,' he often says, when the guests have all been given their glasses. At that point, what am I supposed to do? Early on, I made the mistake of lingering, supposing that having accepted a glass of wine I was required to join in the conversation. I remember the occasion so well: the local architect was there to discuss renovations to the old barn, along with his wife, not an English-speaker, and her brother. Nobody knew each other very well in those days, so I saw fit to fill the rather awkward silence with some comment upon the pleasantness of the weather. As nobody leapt in to follow up my lead, I took it upon myself to compare the climate of Provence with that of Morecambe where, I explained, I had spent so many of my childhood holidays. Possibly I let my tongue run away with me a little, in striving to be helpful, for I remember describing my fondness for whelks. I went on to recall the time I fell off the pier and was rescued by the famous comedian who was starring in the summer show that year. The very thought of all this made me laugh, of course, and it took me some time to realise I was the only one laughing. The three French guests looked completely bemused, and Mr Gerald and Mr Arthur, behind tight little smiles, seemed to be gritting their teeth. Then Mr Gerald came up to me and in a low, urgent voice suggested it was time I began preparing the dinner. I left the room with all the dignity I could muster, as Mr Arthur began to speak to the guests in French, no doubt explaining my extraordinary behaviour.

I have to say, nothing was said. They did not reprove me. And after that, when wine was being served, one of them would bring a glass to me in the kitchen. Well, I got the message: I did not take offence – I'm not one to take offence, it's so time-consuming. I had learned my humiliating lesson and thereafter strove to be the essence of tact. I also realised at that time that there was no question of Mr Gerald and Mr Arthur *ever* being intimates: while they were rarely anything but friendly, they would never be friends. It was necessary to them to keep their distance.

They liked the protection of formality and it was not my place to try to persuade them to behave in any other way. 'Despite the small grumbles, Annie,' my sister once wrote from Barnet, 'you sound very happy. Mr Gerald and Mr Arthur's formal ways of speaking and so on seem to have had their influence on you, too, if you don't mind my saying so. Do you realise you write in a very grand way now? You use lots of new grand words and complicated sentences these days. It's hardly ever you break into your old way of writing.' I had not realised that, though Mr Arthur and Mr Gerald's way of describing the simplest things had always intrigued me. They were elegant in their use of language. Had this really had some influence on my own writing? It was quite a thought. 'It must mean you admire them,' my sister added.

This, my eleventh summer here, has been unusually hot. Mr Gerald and Mr Arthur have never quite accustomed themselves to the heat, and they react badly. They both become short-tempered, petulant, though they do their best to disguise this state. They change their minds a good deal, and give me conflicting orders, all of which is very taxing as the sweat pours down my face in the kitchen. But I try to keep my calm, and reassure them cooler weather must be on its way. Of course, neither of them is getting any younger. In the unkind light of the midday sun I notice that their hair, identical pure white now, is also similar in its thinness. They puff it over their shining pink temples in an effort to make it look thicker than it really is. Mr Arthur goes a funny colour, sometimes, after lunch, and extends his afternoon siesta by at least an hour. Mr Gerald has become fanatical about his pills – vitamins of every kind – and only takes very short walks these days, always with his stick. Time hasn't been particularly kind to me, either: I've inherited my mother's arthritis in the knee, which keeps me awake many hours of the night. And my childhood migraines come back from time to time. But I keep these things to myself. If Mr Arthur and Mr Gerald thought there was any danger of my cracking up, heaven knows what they would do. I may inadvertently irritate them, but I am their prop, their life-blood, their absolute necessity.

Two days ago the mistral began. I've learned to dread the mistral. It's the only thing that makes me seriously contemplate returning to Morecambe for my retirement. All the stories about its weird and unsettling effects are true. As soon as the wind begins to tug at the trees and beat hotly against my window at night, I feel my blood rise. Anxieties turn my skin to gooseflesh. I try to be reasonable, work out what they are about, but they remain nameless. I find it hard to be myself. Mr Arthur and Mr Gerald are affected, too. Their appetites go, and they snap at one another and spend more time on their telephones. 'We must all brace ourselves, Mr Arthur Mr Gerald,' I say. 'It affects us all the same,' I say, and they slam their doors.

The wind started up with its familiar tugging and snapping, blowing my skirts into warm billows above my knees when I go to hang out the washing. It sneaks through any door left open for a moment, ruffling papers and blowing things to the floor. For a few hours I took a positive attitude: the relief, I thought, of a light breeze to stir the heavy heat we had had for so many weeks. But in truth the mistral is not so much light as malevolent. Its aim is to taunt, to goad, to drive you mad. Well, it's not going to beat me, I told myself, as I slammed shut the kitchen window and scooped up the pile of flour I had arranged on the table for my dough. 'One of God's little tricks sent to try us,' I said to Mr Arthur and Mr Gerald at breakfast. Their temples shone with sweat. They answered with silence.

At lunch I could see that both gentlemen were agitated. I put the pot of chicken casserole on the table, then took up a plate to help Mr Arthur first, as I always did.

'I couldn't eat anything hot on a day like this,' he said, and wiped at his forehead with a silk handkerchief.

'But we always start casseroles in late September, Mr Arthur,' I reminded him.

'I tell you, I can't eat a bloody casserole in this heat. I'll have bread and cheese and fruit.'

He looked quite flushed and Mr Gerald, I noticed, was pulling at his earlobe, a habit he has whenever he is out of sorts.

'Don't you worry yourself, now, Mr Arthur,' I said, cool as anything, determined not to be offended by his rejection of my casserole. 'It won't take me a moment to run you up a nice tomato—'

'Did you hear what I said, Mrs Hawker, woman? I'll have cheese and fruit so you can stuff your infuriating concern . . .' He trailed off, picked up a length of bread.

Of all the offensive elements in his response, it was the word 'woman' that got me most, cut me to the quick. *Woman*! Indicating chattel, inferior, nuisance. *Woman*! Never had I been so insulted in all my years here. But I quickly took a hold on myself. No point in shouting back. It was, after all, the mistral that acted like some devil within him.

'And you, Mr Gerald?' I asked, plunging the ladle into the casserole. 'You'll have some, will you?'

'Just a little, Mrs Hawker. Thank you.'

It was a silent lunch. Mr Arthur left before the coffee, his fine poplin shirt darkened with patches of sweat. Mr Gerald anxiously watched him go.

'It's this heat,' he said, by way of conciliation.

'It gets us all down, Mr Gerald.'

'Quite.'

Once I had poured his coffee he stood up and said he would take it to his room. I suppose he no more wanted to be alone with me than I wanted to be alone with him. In this kind of atmosphere it was safer for all of us to be on our own.

'Mr Arthur will be hungry by tonight, at least,' he said with a very faint smile, which I took to be an apology for his friend's behaviour.

'We'll have cold collations,' I reassured him. 'Don't you worry.'

'Thank you, Mrs Hawker. That would be advisable.'

Once he had gone I continued to sit at the kitchen table, stirring my coffee. I could hear footsteps on stone floors, several doors banging. I could hear shouting, though the words were not clear. Then all was quiet. Just the buzzing of several flies and the snip, snip, snip of the wind against the warm stone of the outside walls.

I don't know how long I sat there listening to the frayed

rhythms of the wind. But eventually, true to habit, I stirred myself to clear the table and wash up. Then I went out into the garden. There, the fig and peach trees were tossing restlessly about, their great heads of silvery leaves trying to dodge the nagging and the teasing of the wind. Their usually calm shade was broken into a thousand moving pieces. Butterflies, driven from their resting places, were tossed in the air like tiny sailing boats on an invisible rough sea, and bees clung tightly to the lavender, silent in their concentration. I walked to the edge of the grounds to where the huge oak tree guarded the precipice. Its branches moved slightly, and its leaves snarled, but it acted with none of the frenzy of the fruit trees. It had learned to resist, I thought. I looked down into the great bowl of a valley where fields of lavender and corn dipped and swayed, confusing the bee-eaters. And overhead clouds scurried like lemmings in a dark blue sky. My skirts whipped about my legs. My hair lashed my face. There was not a moment's stillness. I felt so sad, so profoundly, inexplicably sad. The idea came to me that all I had to do was take a couple of further steps to be consumed for ever by the blue of the valley.

When eventually I returned to the kitchen I found, to my horror, that Mr Arthur and Mr Gerald were seated at the table, thunderous expressions threatening their watches.

'Ah, Mrs Hawker,' said Mr Arthur, all polite sarcasm, 'and what has happened to our tea?'

'It's nearly twenty past four,' said Mr Gerald. 'Very unlike you, Mrs Hawker, to have no tea prepared by now.'

There was a moment's quiet, just the wind still tugging away at the windows. Then I let them have it.

'Fucking hell, *gentlemen*,' I screamed. 'For once, just for once in eleven years I'm ten minutes late with your tea. What a disaster. What a bloody disaster! For you two lazy spoilt selfish slobs, that's a *major* disaster, because you're such hopeless bastards you can't so much as switch on a kettle, fill a pot, fetch the butter from the fridge – do you know which the fridge *is*, Mr Arthur Mr Gerald?'

Perfectly synchronised, their flabby old mouths fell open. But their eyes could not meet, nor could they look at me.

'Aren't you ashamed,' I raved on, 'at your absolute use-lessness, your total inadequacy? You employ me to wait on you hand and foot, do your bidding at every turn: you rely on me completely, useless prats for all your money—'

'Mrs Hawker,' said Mr Arthur.

'Mrs Hawker,' added Mr Gerald.

'Calm yourself.'

'Calm yourself.'

'Calm!'

I fact, I did feel calmer, now. I knew my words would come more tightly, with more menace. 'Who could be calm at the thought of a future waiting on two spoiled old sods? Who could be calm thinking that old age would still be darning your socks, getting your porridge just right while my own life just ebbs away? Course, if you live to bury me, I've no doubt you'll commission a nice marble headstone engraved with the tribute *A good and faithful servant* . . .'

'You've gone too far, Mrs Hawker,' said Mr Arthur, dabbing at the string of sweat on his nose.

'Much too far,' said Mr Gerald, running a finger round his damp collar.

'You're not yourself. The mistral, it affects us all.'

'Not yourself, indeed.'

'Not myself?' I gave a nasty laugh that made them both jump in their seats. 'As a matter of fact, Mr Arthur Mr Gerald, that's just what I am being at this moment – *myself*. For the first time in all these years, *myself*. The bit you've never shown the slightest desire to know about, to see. Well, I've only just begun. Sorry to shock you, but there's much, much more I'd like to say . . .'

I saw a look pass between them, then, and Mr Arthur gave an almost invisible sigh. The words I had ready to shoot at them were exploding in my head in such blinding lights that I could not quite read them – something to do with bitterness at the waste of my life, nothing but the satisfaction of two spoilt old men to show for it: the regret at so meagre an achievement, and the sadness – could they not understand the sadness?

They seemed to be waiting for me to go on. But anger had left me inarticulate. Words, insults, evaporated. So I began to moan, a noise similar to the wind. As I picked up the huge pottery bowl Mr Arthur and Mr Gerald looked scared. I thrust the fruit at them, moaning louder. A brilliant aim: figs caught Mr Arthur on the chest, making smeary pink marks on his clean shirt, and bursting obscenely over his fingers when he put up a hand to shield his face. An over-ripe peach slobbered down Mr Gerald's temple. I laughed again. I picked random crockery from the dresser and began to throw it on to the stone floor. The

shotgun explosions of cups and saucers and the large dinner plates were pure music: pottery breaks into noisy
crumbs. Glass, next. Half a dozen wine glasses landed in
the stainless steel sink. They smashed with a high-pitched
scream, drowning the noise of the wind. Then a jar of
olives – they rolled about the messed-up floor like jet mar-
bles, smearing it with olive oil. The homemade jams: two
large jars, Mr Gerald's favourites, burst on to the floor,
sticky plums sploshing among the olives and china. And
finally the inspiration of a bag of flour. As I picked up a
kitchen knife to slash the bag for speed, Mr Arthur and Mr
Gerald turned a matching deathly white. In a moment they
were whiter still as I held it high and let it scatter down like
a snowstorm. I loved its silent descent into random piles
that covered everything.

'This is . . .' Mr Arthur stood up, a floury spectre. Flour
fell mistily from him.

'. . . too much, Mrs Hawker.' Mr Gerald, still troubled by
peach in his eye, stood up too.

Something told me they were right. Besides, the energy
was ebbing, just as the words had done earlier on.

'If I've caused you just a moment's thought, Mr Arthur
Mr Gerald,' I said, 'then this has been worth it.'

Head very high, I left the room.

That was all some four hours ago. Since then, back in my
room, I've been writing like a lunatic. All this stuff. Giving
vent to, as they say. Letting it all out. As I pause for a
moment I look out of the window and notice the trees are
still. A bee-eater on the telegraph wires, eyes speared on to

the lavender bush below, does not sway. The wind has died. Only the scratching of my pen in the silence.

Then the buzzer goes, frightening. I pick up the telephone.

'Mrs Hawker? It's almost eight o'clock.'

'So it is, Mr Arthur,' I say.

'Dinner-time,' he says.

'I'll be along, Mr Arthur.'

I stand, stretch. It's one of those dusky blue evenings I love so much. The crickets will start up again now the wind has gone. Funny how much I've enjoyed the writing. The hours just flew. Perhaps I shall try it again. Perhaps that's how I shall spend my time off in my old age, writing stories at last. I brush a streak of flour from my sleeve. I am very calm.

In the kitchen Mr Gerald is laying the table – three places. Very unusual, for I only dine with them at Christmas and on my birthday. He wears one of my aprons. Candles are lighted. A bottle of good wine is open. Over at the oven Mr Arthur is prodding expertly at the chicken casserole and tossing a salad. There's no sign that anything untoward (a favourite word of Mr Gerald's) has ever taken place. China and glass from the cupboard have replaced the missing things on the dresser. There's a bowl of olives – one of them must have been down to the village to buy more – and the flour jar is filled. What an afternoon they must have had! I try not to smile. I say nothing.

'Sit down, Annie,' says Mr Arthur, back to me.

'It's our turn to wait on you, Annie,' says Mr Gerald, without looking at me.

I do as they ask, and we have the dinner of a lifetime.

Now, it's past midnight. Even as I finish this story I find it hard to believe it all happened. The merging of fact and fiction in memory, however soon after the event, is intriguing. How much of what I have described was exactly like that? I have tried to be accurate, but if someone were to ask Mr Arthur and Mr Gerald to describe the events of today, some years from now, I've no doubt they would tell quite a different story. What I do know is that everyone is entitled to such terrible days now and then, and that, in the end, is what Mr Arthur and Mr Gerald understood, and that's why I love them and will work for them for the rest of my days.

Besides, they called me Annie. Of course – and I must stop now, I'm feeling suddenly tired – I know that was only for tonight. Mrs Hawker is how they like me to be, and why not? So Mrs Hawker I'll be again in the morning. But at least I have been Annie for a night.

I set my alarm.

Men Friends

Conrad Fortescue, on his way into the church, trod on a beetle. In the silence of the Norman porch he heard the tiny crackle as it crushed beneath his foot. Looking down, he saw the smashed shell, each fragment shiny as his own highly polished black shoes, linked by a web of blood. Damn, he thought: how Louisa would have hated this – Louisa who would rescue dying flies from summer window-panes. Conrad felt his throat clench. He coughed. Up until this moment he had been all right, in control. Death of the beetle shattered his calm.

He made his way into the church. He was early. Walking up the path banked with expensive wreaths of flowers at the foot of the yews, he had been pleased to think he was probably the first. He wanted time to himself to think about Louisa. But he was not the first. Half a dozen others were already seated, curious vulture eyes upon him, people behaving as if the gathering was for a party rather than a funeral. Conrad took a service sheet from an usher, chose a seat by a pillar from which he would not quite be able to see the coffin. *Louisa Chumleigh*, he read: *1st Sept 1956 – 2nd April 1992*. Not a long life. The organ began to play a Bach prelude. Conrad closed his eyes.

They first met seven years ago, one of those smudged

summer afternoons when the tremor of heat makes every-thing illusory. He stood on a thyme-planted terrace, leaning over the balustrade to admire the descending shelves of impeccably mowed lawns. Friends had brought him to the house for tea, drinks – he couldn't remember which. He had stood transfixed as he watched Louisa, in the shimmer of heat below him, take the arm of an old man with a stick. She supported him as he stepped from the lawn on to the path. Her solicitousness – she had no idea she was being watched, she later told him – was mirage-clear even from so great a distance. She kept hold of the old man's arm – Jacob, it was, her husband. They walked towards Conrad, joined him on the terrace. As Jacob pointed his stick towards the arboretum, spoke lovingly of trees, Conrad regarded his wife. It was a case of instant enchantment. Something unknown to him before.

They had had five years. Five years of adultery, though Louisa would never use such a word. She had made it easy for him – writing, ringing, taking the initiative to get in touch, so that he was spared taking the risk of contacting her. She never involved him in her deceits. She even man-aged to make him feel, sometimes, that the woman in his arms was *free*. But that was the one thing she was not, nor ever would be until Jacob died. Until that time, her hus-band came first. If she did not ring Conrad for a week – and the agony of silent days never lessened – he knew it would be because Jacob had made some demand that she would not dream of refusing, although when she did ring she gave no explanation for her silence. And Conrad knew better than to ask.

Once, they had managed three whole days together: Jacob was on business in America. Louisa took the opportunity to visit relations in Paris. Conrad followed her on the next flight. Louisa saw little of her relations. On a warm spring afternoon in the Bois, Conrad declared his intention to wait for her: to wait until Jacob, thirty-six years her senior, died. He saw at once his mistake. Louisa, who had been laughing only moments before, retracted from him, though she kept hold of his hand. Conrad, apologising for his clumsiness, felt a lowering of the afternoon. 'Who knows what will happen – then?' Louisa said. 'It's something I can never think about, Jacob's dying.'

Soon she was laughing again. Back in England nothing seemed to have changed. Conrad accustomed himself to the imperfections of loving another man's wife, and privately determined to wait, however many years it might be.

Then, two years ago, there had been such a long silence that Conrad had been forced at last to write. What had happened? Louisa rang at once, her weak voice apologetic. Some wretched bug, she explained. She hadn't wanted to worry him. She had been forced to stay in bed for two weeks.

The bug needed treatment – radiotherapy. Conrad visited her occasionally when Jacob was away. He observed her thinning, beautiful skin gleaming with an incandescent menace. Noticeably more frail each visit, she lay back against a bank of linen pillows in the huge marital bedroom whose windows looked on to the garden. Conrad would look down on the lawns, misted with rain, and see the brilliance of that first summer day. A nurse filtered in and out, filling water jugs, straightening covers. Conrad brought pansies, in which Louisa silently buried her face, and elderberry jelly. She spread it thinly on toast, but could only eat a mouthful to please him. They held hands, talked about the past. But mostly sat in silence watching the rain on vast window-panes. Sometimes, Louisa felt like being up for a while. Once they walked down to the lake and back, which exhausted her.

Conrad learned of her death in *The Times*. None of their mutual friends knew of their affair so, not surprisingly, offered no condolences. He had written at once to Jacob, who replied by return, a stiff polite letter in an infirm hand, inviting Conrad to the funeral and lunch afterwards at the house.

Now Louisa was dead, Conrad would never marry. She was the only woman in whom he had found all the qualities he had never known he needed until he found them in her. He doubted he would ever love anyone else.

The church was filling up: men in black ties, women in dark hats. A large man with extraordinarily wide shoulders sat in front of Conrad, uncomfortable on the narrow bench of the pew, shifting about. Conrad recognised Johnnie Lutchins, a childhood friend. Louisa had sometimes talked about their times together in Cornwall.

Cornwall, Scotland, the south-west of Ireland – Johnnie and Louisa had spent many holidays together. Johnnie's widowed mother had been the best friend of Louisa's mother. She and her son spent much of their time with Louisa's family. Johnnie remembered his first sight of Louisa, a skinny angel in filthy dungarees. *Feeble*, he remembered thinking, at ten: but within the day he had discovered she was tough and daring as any boy. They climbed trees, sailed in brisk seas – the rougher the better, Louisa used to say. They teased an old donkey, put pretend spiders in the cook's tea – always laughing, always daring the other into greater mischief. At fifteen, Johnnie kissed Louisa in the greenhouse among unripe tomatoes. Then he couldn't stop kissing her. When he went up to Oxford three years later, she would visit him several times a term. He was the envy of all his friends, and showed off the beautiful creature at every opportunity. After he had graduated, and found a decent job in antiquarian books, he finally declared his love and proposed. But he had been beaten to it by Jacob – Jacob, a man older than Louisa's own father. When Johnnie had recovered from the shock, he had tried to dissuade her from such madness. Then he had turned to teasing. 'I can only conclude you're marrying the old boy for his money and his house,' he had laughed, bitterly. Louisa denied this. Neither Johnnie nor anyone could stop her from becoming Jacob's wife.

Still, as Johnnie soon found to his delight, the marital state made little difference to their friendship. Jacob, who had known Johnnie since he was a boy – indeed, he was Johnnie's godfather – issued constant invitations to the house. Johnnie was urged to look after Louisa, keep her amused, when Jacob was away on business. Which meant that with a half-clear conscience they could go out together in London. Opportunity was on their side: Johnnie considered himself the luckiest man in the world. He knew Louisa loved him, even if not in quite the same way as he loved her. It was only a matter of waiting . . . sometimes she had frustrated him by her silences, but he knew they meant she was being dutiful to Jacob, and he had no right to be either impatient or greedy. When she had become ill he had spent hours, days, by her bedside, laughing at the many flowers and cards sent to her by 'admirers' whom, she claimed, she hardly knew. Johnnie believed her.

He saw her on the day before she died – asleep, but holding Jacob's hand. The old man sat with fresh tears replacing dried tears on his cheeks, making no effort to brush them away. But when he rang Johnnie next morning with the news, his voice was firm as usual. He was a digni- fied old boy. He would have been horrified by Johnnie's uncontrolled weeping.

To deflect his thoughts, Johnnie glanced round the church. Hundreds of pansies were woven into ivy round the pillars, and along ledges where they mixed with the reflections of stained-glass windows, and twined into edi- fices on the altar. Candles burned as if it were Christmas Eve. The pews were full. People were hunting for seats in the side aisles. Many of them resigned themselves to stand- ing. One of those, Johnnie realised, was Bernard Wylie. Johnnie had met him and Louisa one day in Bond Street, very briefly. He had only just caught the name. Later, he remembered to ask Louisa about him. She said Wylie was a solicitor – something to do with her late father's affairs. They had both laughed about the slickness of his coat, with its too-wide velvet collar. Today, Johnnie recognised the coat before the face.

Bernard Wylie wore his favourite coat accompanied by

expensive black leather gloves, and a black satin tie lightened with the tiniest white spots which he had judged would not be offensive. He stood clutching his service sheet to steady his hands, staring straight ahead, feeling the uncertainty of his knees. And he wondered for the millionth time what it was about Louisa that had so bewitched him that his life, since meeting her, had fallen apart.

She had come into his office one November afternoon – some trivial matter to do with her father's estate – wearing a hat of grey fur sparkling with rain. Completely confused by the legal niceties of the matter, she had suddenly said, 'Oh, I give up, Mr Wylie,' and had laughed her enchanting laugh. 'In that case,' he had said, 'let's go and have tea while I explain it all to you very slowly.'

So slowly that their tea at the Ritz drifted into champagne, and then dinner. He had driven her back to her flat, come in for a drink, stayed the night. There had been dozens of nights since – nights and lunches, little notes and presents from her, calls from all parts of the world when she was travelling with Jacob. Then, a year or so before she fell ill, there was the final note. 'I'm awfully sorry, darling B, but we can't go on. I realise now it was all *infatuation* on my part . . . and know it was not real love for you either, but great fun, and thank you.'

For the rest of his life, Bernard would regret not having made his declaration – Christ, he had loved her from the moment she walked into his office. But he had bided by Byron's principle of never telling your love, merely conveying it. Had his conveying been invisible? Too late he wrote to her, pages of the long-contained passion now set free. But she did not reply. The last time he saw her was at a party, laughing in the distance with some unknown man. She had not seen him. Bernard had left at once.

And now instead of Louisa he had a second-best wife at his side who would never know the loving man he once was . . . She nudged him, this loyal, unexciting wife, her sense of occasion offended by the sight of a young man standing not far from them in a dark jacket, grey trousers and no tie. In the unknown youth's eye, Bernard thought he saw reflected the same despair that lodged in his own heart: but it may have been his imagination.

The young man, Felix Brown, had cried for many nights. Cold, exhausted, drained, he feared he might faint during the long service, but there were no seats left. He it was who late last night, and at dawn this morning, had transported pansies from the greenhouse to the church, and arranged them on his own. Only three years ago, Lady Endlesham – as he still thought of her, as he would always think of her – had come into that very greenhouse and admired them. Said they were her favourite flowers. They had talked of planting and pruning, and made plans for the south bed. Felix had done his best to conceal the mesmeric effect the shape of her breasts beneath a pink cotton shirt had had upon him. He had told her how happy he was to be working in the garden. He could scarcely believe he had been promoted to being in charge only two years after leaving horticultural college, he said. Lady Endlesham had smiled, and said they must make more plans. Then he gave her a pot of pansies for her desk.

Some weeks later she came into the tool-shed, admired

his clean and gleaming tools that hung in order of height on the walls. The warmth of that evening was almost tangible. In the stuffy air that smelt of dry earth Felix was embarrassed by the pungent smell of his own sweat. He could also smell Lady Endlesham's scent, a mixture of fragile flowers. In the shadows it seemed to him she hesitated, planning perhaps to mention some gardening matter. Then she put out her arms, and said, he thought – though he could never be quite sure of the exact words – *Come here, you handsome thing.* Handsome? Gathered to him, Felix could hear the racing heart of his employer's wife. They ran like children through the orchard to a hidden place Felix knew. Lord Endlesham was away, she assured him, but not in a rejoicing way. She sounded almost lonely. Felix was twenty-one at the time.

Since then they'd made love in every corner of the garden, and, in winter, in the hayloft. Felix would marvel how one moment his mistress (as he liked to think of her) was laughing in his arms covered in grass or hay, and the next he would see her in the distance walking beside her aged husband, immaculate, admiring the flowerbeds whose geography she and Felix had discussed between a thousand kisses.

When she was ill, no longer able to come downstairs, he sent up a new bowl of flowers to her room each day. The last time he saw her she was standing at her bedroom window – looking for him, perhaps. He was raking the terrace. He glanced up, saw her wave. Then she disappeared. She disappeared, and with a crescendo in the organ music Felix knew at last she was gone. Never coming back to their garden. He took out his handkerchief, blew his nose, realising he was the only man in the church to resort to such weakness at this stage. Through tear-blurred eyes he watched the shuffling procession of coffin-bearers hesitate up the aisle, and caught the eye of his employer, Sir Jacob, seventy-two at Christmas. He was a good man to work for. Felix respected the old codger, but wondered if he could bear to continue the job now the inspiration of the garden no longer existed.

Sir Jacob, seeing young Felix, the first face to come clearly into focus, gave the briefest nod to acknowledge that his floral work in the church was appreciated. Louisa would have been amazed. She loved decorating the church. She and Felix, before the illness, had done a grand job always at Christmas and Harvest Festival. She had been wonderful with the boy. In her usual generous way she had inspired him, encouraged him, suggested his promotion – typical of her, always seeing the best in people, bringing out their qualities.

Sir Jacob trod very slowly, in time to the gentle music. In front of him on the coffin lay a single gardenia. He had chosen it with Felix – the best in the greenhouse. Inside, placed in the stiff hands, was the equally stiff card with its private message of love which would not fade until long after the body had perished.

Beside Sir Jacob walked Louisa's mother, a bent old lady with a still-beautiful profile that had been inherited by her daughter. It occurred to Sir Jacob, as he put a finger on the knife-edge of his collar that cut into his neck, that they might look more like man and wife than he and Louisa ever did . . . Louisa could have been his granddaughter.

Walking down this same aisle, their wedding day – but he hadn't cared then, or ever, what people thought. All that mattered to him was their mutual, perfect love for each other. Which turned out to be proven. While Sir Jacob recoiled at the thought of his own smugness, he couldn't help reflecting that never once in their sixteen years of marriage had Louisa ever let him down, disappointed him, betrayed him. He knew he came first in her life, just as she did in his. He had trusted her absolutely. The only worry they had ever had was about her life after his death. She often said that no one ever could replace him.

The coffin-bearers reached the altar, placed it on its plinth. Sir Jacob and his mother-in-law took their places in the front pew. A shaft of sun, at that moment, pierced the roseate glass of the window above the altar. Sir Jacob remembered Louisa remarking on the strength of its colour – 'a small pink pool on the altar steps, darling – did you notice?' In truth he had never noticed, in all the Sundays he had been coming to this church, until Louisa had pointed it out to him. She had drawn so much to his attention that gave pleasure. She had opened his eyes to the extraordinary qualities of the ordinary, and made him the happiest of men.

The vicar clasped his hands. In the moment's silence before the first prayer, Sir Jacob looked round at the congregation – so many people who would always remember his wife. It occurred to him there was a large proportion of men. Men of all ages, he saw, all with that sternness of eye that strong men employ to conceal grief. He knew some of them: others were unfamiliar. Darling Louisa: untouchable to all but me, he used to say. And she, kneeling on the library floor beside him, would laugh her thrilling laugh in agreement. How proud of her he was! There was nothing like having a wife who was desired by all, but faithful only to the man she loved, her husband.

May the vanity of such thoughts be forgiven, Sir Jacob found himself praying. Then he joined in the general words of thanks for Louisa's life. He could not close his eyes: in his disbelief they never left the coffin. Like so many of Louisa's men friends in the church for her funeral that day, Sir Jacob could only picture her alive.

LAND GIRLS

Angela Huth

'Piquant, witty and entertaining'
Tatler

The West Country in wartime, and the land girls are
gathering on the farm of John and Faith Lawrence.

Prue, a man-eating hairdresser from Manchester; Ag, a
cerebral Cambridge undergraduate; and Stella, a dreamy
Surrey girl stunted by love: three very different women,
from very different backgrounds, who find themselves
thrown together, sharing an attic bedroom and laying the
foundations for a friendship that will last a lifetime.

'Angela Huth's riveting novel . . . is evocative and
entertaining'
Mail on Sunday

'It had me in its grip and I couldn't rest until the final
page . . . It is satisfying and rare to read a book whose
characters are dealt the fates we feel they deserve . . . A
beautifully spun tale that absorbs without the need to
address "issues"'
Literary Review

'A good story, told with wit and a keen observation of
detail'
Times Literary Supplement

Abacus
0 349 10601 0

VIRGINIA FLY IS DROWNING

Angela Huth

Quiet, clever, sensible Virginia Fly, still a virgin at
thirty-one, harbours erotic thoughts of an intensity and
vividness unimagined by her suburban parents, her
unassuming elderly suitor Hans or even her virile
American penfriend of twelve years, Charles Whitmore
Oakhampton Jr. – Charlie.

When Charlie announces that he is, at last, to visit
England, it seems too much to hope that he should make
Virginia's dreams of passion reality. Yet his arrival
coincides with her appearance on a television documentary
and suddenly Virginia is presented with a bewildering
variety of opportunities to rid herself of her virginity. The
only question remaining seems to be whether any of them
– even the sauve and delicious stranger Ulick Brand –
could possibly fulfil her considerable expectations.

'A sharply etched study . . . sly comedy'
Mail on Sunday

Abacus
0 349 10672 X

<u>INVITATION TO THE MARRIED LIFE</u>

Angela Huth

'I was completely betwitched by it. I think there is a very strong case for Huth replacing Jane Austen on the school syllabus'
Sunday Times

The married couples in this book have two things in common: a skill in the duplicity that flourishes even in happy marriages, and an invitation to the Farthingoes' Ball . . .

'It should become a classic . . . wonderfully quick and funny about the sheer unfairness of the sexual emotions, and how this affects the orthodox patterns of married life . . . a comic and beautiful climax'
Evening Standard

'Angela Huth unsheathes a wicked wit behind her gentleness and gentility . . . and she writes with verve and love. You identify so well with her characters that you long for the pleasure of everyone's company at the ball. You won't be disappointed'
Mail on Sunday

Abacus
0 349 10313 5

NOWHERE GIRL

Angela Huth

'A first-class writer'
Sunday Telegraph

Estranged from her second husband Jonathan, Clare Lyall
is less sure than ever about the role men should play in
her life.

Her first husband, Richard, was much older than her, and
his casual disregard for youth gradually hardened into
indifference. And Jonathan, if anything, was too easy – too
attentive, too concerned, and just a little too pedantic.

So when she meets Joshua Heron at a party, the offbeat
Clare isn't exactly thirsting for love. But she is mildly
impressed when Joshua stubs his cigarette out on his
thumb, and swayed still further by the advice of her new
friend, the indomitable Mrs Fox. 'Take a lover,' she says,
'it's better to have a lover when you're young than neurosis
when you're old . . .'

'Angela Huth is an excellent exponent of the traditional
English social comedy.'
Daily Telegraph

Abacus
0 349 10630 4

SOUTH OF THE LIGHTS

Angela Huth

South of the Lights weaves the story of Evans and Brenda, lovers in a Midlands village, whose happiest hours are spent in the hayloft of the chicken farm on which she works. They have no other roof under which they can be alone together – until the mysterious, romantic Augusta comes to their aid. Evans' desire to possess Brenda results sometimes in passion, sometimes in violence, but Brenda finds sympathy in the company of the fragile and sweet-natured Lark with whom she shares a flat in the local town.

Excelling in the illumination of the surprising facets of people's daily lives, Angela Huth reveals their private hopes, rages, fantasies and despair, with an original and moving blend of humour, imagination and pathos.

'Comical . . . English village life of the late 1970s yields to Huth's wicked scalpel a gruesome mix of bleak and racy secrets'
The Times

Abacus
0 349 10554 5

JANE GARDAM

Faith Fox

'Terribly funny and clever . . . the best thing she's done'
Victoria Wood

When sweet, healthy, hearty Holly Fox dies suddenly in
childbirth, the Surrey village whose pearl she was
reverberates with shock. She leaves behind her a helpless,
silent husband, and a tiny daughter, Faith. Everyone
assumes Holly's loving and capable mother Thomasina
will look after Faith, but when she unaccountably deserts
her newborn grandchild, the baby must be packed off to
her father's peculiar family in the North – 'the very
strangest people you ever saw, my dear'. With wisdom,
generosity and understanding, Jane Gardam takes as her
subject the English heart in all its eccentric variety. *Faith
Fox* sheds a clear, true light on the misery of bereavement
and the joyous possibility of a new beginning.

'*Faith Fox* has quite as sharp a take on modern times as
Trainspotting . . . if you're too hip for Jane Gardam, then
you're too hip'
D. J. Taylor, *New Statesman*

'Funny and admirable . . . Jane Gardam writes with a
dark and buoyant energy which continually challenges
and provokes'
The Times

'Dazzling . . . Funny, bleak and full of wisdom, *Faith Fox* is
a complete delight'
Marie Claire

'She has Alan Bennett's gift of bringing out the hubris,
and, simultaneously, the humility of her characters, who
are an endearing lot'
Guardian

Abacus
0 349 10823 4

BLACK FACES, WHITE FACES

Jane Gardam

'Extraordinary . . . Jane Gardam is a writer of original
spirit, her observations acute and funny/sad'
Angela Huth, *Guardian*

In this loosely connected sequence of short stories, Jane
Gardam offers dazzling vignettes of human foibles in the
smilingly fierce holiday island of Jamaica. Mrs Filling sees
something nasty in the midday sun; an English lawyer
dallies with Mrs Santamania the Bolivian Queen while his
wife goes quietly mad in England; an ancient American
silenced by a stroke is tortured by the ramblings of his
wife. Years of studiously correct behaviour in a colder
climate give way to astonishing desires; middle-aged ladies
appear in the wrong clothes; sexuality flares towards the
wrong partners, and everywhere terror, farce and
undercurrents of racial tension lurk beside the
swimming pool.

'Jane Gardam has taken the form of the short story as close
to art as it is ever likely to reach'
Peter Ackroyd, *Spectator*

'Very good indeed . . . she writes so well'
Victoria Glendinning

'She writes like a modern Katherine Mansfield . . . a
little gem'
Daily Mail

Abacus
0 349 11407 2

YESTERDAY IN THE BACK LANE

Bernice Rubens

'Wonderfully compelling'
Spectator

Yesterday, just before a war-time Christmas, Bronwen
Davies became a murderess.

Quieting the desire of the man she meets in the back lane
near her Cardiff terrace, she hides the deed under a veil of
shame, watching the tainted knife carve her family's festive
turkey. It is a matter for her conscience alone, a sin to
carry with her in silence. Bronwen knows her confession
could save an innocent man from the gallows, but
self-sacrifice demands a special kind of courage and she's
just an ordinary girl; prone to nose-bleeds at awkward
moments, and proud of her well-defended virginity.

Now, after fifty years of yesterdays, Bronwen is still living
her life sentence.

'A moving tale, but not without vivid comic relief . . .
captures the human condition and the constraints we place
upon ourselves with graphic intensity'
Observer

'Rubens combines a sharply observant eye with a
sympathetic psychological understanding . . . She writes
like a dream. Nothing could be bettered in this most
excellent novel'
Evening Standard

'Bernice Rubens is a novelist to be treasured'
The Times

Abacus
0 349 10763 7

THAT BAD WOMAN

Clare Boylan

'Sharp, witty, and irresistibly brilliant'
Independent

Focusing on the dilemmas of contemporary women and
issues of responsibility and choice, Clare Boylan's
collection of short stories illuminates with pathos and
perception the potential of thwarted ordinary women and
the mismatched yearnings of the men who subdue them.
Graced with both humour and compassion, *That Bad
Woman* bewitches as it unsettles, confirming Clare Boylan's
ability to subvert our reactions with irony as keen and deft
as a surgeon's blade.

'These are songs of innocence and experience, the kind you
hear when you're walking down the street and remember
for a long time afterwards'
The Times

'Truly wonderful stories. The words sing on the page.
Clare Boylan is in a league of her own'
Deborah Moggach

'Outstanding'
Sunday Telegraph

'Boylan . . . can beat Weldon hands down for savage
comedy, clever writing and her ability to evoke the
complexities of human psychology'
Irish Times

Abacus
0 349 10737 8

☐	Land Girls	Angela Huth	£6.99
☐	Virginia Fly is Drowning	Angela Huth	£6.99
☐	Invitation to the Married Life	Angela Huth	£6.99
☐	Nowhere Girl	Angela Huth	£6.99
☐	South of the Lights	Angela Huth	£6.99
☐	Faith Fox	Jane Gardam	£6.99
☐	Black Faces, White Faces	Jane Gardam	£5.99
☐	Yesterday in the Back Lane	Bernice Rubens	£6.99
☐	That Bad Woman	Clare Boylan	£6.99

Abacus now offers an exciting range of quality titles by both established and new authors. All of the books in this series are available from:

Little, Brown and Company (UK),
P.O. Box 11,
Falmouth,
Cornwall TR10 9EN.
Telephone No: 01326 317200
Fax No: 01326 317444
E-mail: books@barni.avel.co.uk

Payments can be made as follows: cheque, postal order (payable to Little, Brown and Company) or by credit cards, Visa/Access. Do not send cash or currency. UK customers and B.F.P.O. please allow £1.00 for postage and packing for the first book, plus 50p for the second book, plus 30p for each additional book up to a maximum charge of £3.00 (7 books plus).

Overseas customers including Ireland, please allow £2.00 for the first book plus £1.00 for the second book, plus 50p for each additional book.

NAME (Block Letters) ....

....

ADDRESS ....

....

....

☐ I enclose my remittance for ....
☐ I wish to pay by Access/Visa Card

Number ☐☐☐☐☐☐☐☐☐☐☐☐☐☐☐☐

Card Expiry Date ☐☐☐☐